WATCH MY BACK

WATCH MY BACK

From a Montana ranch to Rio's beaches and slums, four men learn that being in danger is the best thing to ever happen to them.

Previously available only in electronic format, these two sizzling stories of Gay Erotic Romance have now been combined for a paperback edition! Included are the tales...

Under A Rock

When his father crossed a powerful Mexican drug cartel, Keith Lewis lost everything. He never expected to find something better on an isolated Montana ranch. Keith isn't the first witness to shelter in Tanner Bruenig's house, but he may be the first one Tanner wants to keep there.

Blood On The Mountain

Being chased through the slums of one of the most glamorous cities on Earth, hiding from drug lords in the very shacks and hovels he had come to replace, Nathan Graves realizes that getting to know Gabe Callan better will have to take a back seat to getting home alive.

WATCH MY BACK

BY

INDIA HARPER

AMBER QUILL PRESS, LLC
http://www.amberquill.com

WATCH MY BACK
AN AMBER QUILL PRESS BOOK

This book is a work of fiction. All names, characters, locations, and incidents are products of the author's imagination, or have been used fictitiously. Any resemblance to actual persons living or dead, locales, or events is entirely coincidental.

Amber Quill Press, LLC
http://www.amberquill.com

Copyright © 2011 by India Harper
ISBN 978-1-61124-935-4
Cover Art © 2011 Trace Edward Zaber

Layout and Formatting provided by: ElementalAlchemy.com

PUBLISHED IN THE UNITED STATES OF AMERICA

TABLE OF CONTENTS

UNDER A ROCK

WATCH MY BACK

CHAPTER 1

Keith hunkered down in the passenger seat of the rented Cherokee, determined not to be sick despite the constant jouncing from the potted, worn-out, two-track road they were following. "How much farther?"

Marta Collins grinned over at him from behind the wheel, her sunglasses hiding her eyes. "What's the matter, Mr. Martin? Getting tired of my company?"

"What I'm getting tired of, Marshal, is all the damn traveling. In the past two weeks, I've been in Sandusky, Mobile, Knoxville, Salt Lake and some podunk town in Colorado I never even got the name of. And now you're driving me out into some godforsaken corner of Montana in a car that needed new shocks about twenty thousand miles ago. There had better be a four-star hotel at the end of this road."

She snorted. "Keep dreaming. Unless you really do want your head hanging on the Escavera cartel's wall."

Marta had been the one constant in his life—such as it was anymore—since this whole mess started. She was efficient and brilliant, but Christ, did she have a dark sense of humor sometimes. If you can't laugh at the shit life throws at you, what's the point? was her favorite motto.

"It's not like any of this is my fault. How do we even know if any of them are after me?"

"Honey"—she risked the perils of the road long enough to glare at him over the top of her shades—"your daddy was one of the most prominent attorneys in Houston. And you, Mr. Playboy, made sure you were known far and wide as his charming heir. With Daddy turning state's evidence to avoid some rather serious racketeering charges against some even more serious Mexican drug families, I'd say you're right at the top of the list of people the Escaveras would really like to get hold of at the moment."

"Yeah, but I'm beginning to wonder if their accommodations might not be better." The last town was maybe thirty miles back. As for the nearest honest-to-God city, he doubted Montana even had one.

"Shall I pull out the pictures of the last person they *accommodated?*"

Keith's stomach lurched, and not from the ride this time. He hadn't thought it possible to cut the human body into so many pieces.

"Is there indoor plumbing where you're taking me?"

"All the comforts of home."

"If you live in a barn."

"Funny you should say that…"

Rounding the base of a low hill, they came upon a sprawling enclosure with two big barns and a log ranch house someone must have lifted out of a Zane Grey novel, all sitting in the middle of the vast prairie, the Rocky Mountains rising up in the distance. Two pickups and a Land Rover were parked outside the house, and Keith could see a satellite dish perched on one corner of the barn.

"Welcome home, Mr. Martin."

He took in the nothingness surrounding them. "A farm. I'm going to be living on a fucking farm?"

"It's that or in a cesspool being tortured by one of the Escavera lackeys."

"You promise there's indoor plumbing?"

Marta pointed out the satellite dish he'd already noticed. "This may be the sticks, but it's not exactly the Wild West."

A man emerged from the cabin, stocky of build and dressed in worn jeans and a plaid shirt. At least he wasn't wearing a cowboy hat.

He smiled, a warm greeting as they pulled up, opening the door for Marta when she killed the engine. "Glad you found the place."

Marta didn't look put out by his chivalry. Apparently, she didn't need to prove to anyone she was a tough chick. "GPS works even out here in the hinterland. Christ, Tanner, I know you like being away from it all, but I'll never get used to *how* away from it all."

"Yeah." He looked around proudly. "Great, isn't it?"

"You'll have to ask your houseguest. Tanner Bruenig, meet Keith

4

Martin. He's going to be staying with you for a few months."

Tanner gave Keith a once-over and smirked. "Never done any manual labor in your life, have you?"

"I go to the gym. Regularly." Or had gone until all this happened.

"Uh-huh." Tanner and Marta exchanged a look.

"He's from Texas. Texas is like Montana, right?" Marta didn't hide her amusement. "With fewer oil rigs and Mexicans. I like places for Keith with fewer Mexicans."

"You sure won't find many Mexicans up here."

"See? It's the perfect place."

Keith didn't agree. "How about Seattle? I bet there aren't a lot of Mexicans in Seattle. Or Denver. Denver would be good."

"You'd be surprised. And you'll be staying here."

Grumbling to himself, Keith grabbed his duffle bag—why he couldn't have real, proper luggage he just didn't understand—and got out. The sooner he started this masquerade, the sooner it would be over. He hoped.

Despite Tanner's assurances and their extreme isolation, Marta didn't drop her guard for a second, making them both wait on the porch while she checked the house, hand never far from her unsnapped holster. It was only September, but already a chill breeze danced through the air, warning Keith that winter was going to come long before he could get out of here and was going to be a cold and miserable experience. He shivered and hunkered down in his jacket.

Tanner seemed to read his body language. "Relax. It's not as bad as you think it will be. Do you ride?"

"Some. I had lessons when I was a kid, but never did anything competitive."

"As long as you can stay on a horse and aren't afraid of them, you'll do fine. We won't be doing a lot of roping and racing. Just riding the fence lines every couple of days and checking the herds for any surprises."

"Herds?" He looked out again over the empty prairie.

"I've got about eight hundred head of cattle out there grazing, more in the spring and summer before we sell off to market. I have some Native Americans out of Fort Belknap and Rocky Boy working as cowboys, so I don't have to tend the herd, only check up on them."

"Sounds easy enough."

"Ain't nothing easy out here," Tanner said. "Though, if Marta could do it, I think you'll manage."

5

"You better not be insulting me behind my back," Marta called out, emerging soon after. "All clear."

"You expected otherwise?" Tanner sounded offended.

"Sweetie, you may be an ex-Navy SEAL, but you are still human. And this is your home. You'd be surprised what you can miss."

"Not likely. It's not as if there's any place for people to hide trying to sneak up to the house. In case you hadn't noticed, there's a whole lot of nothing out there."

"Just the way I like it. Now are you going to feed us? Or do I have to drive all the way back to Billings on an empty stomach?"

"If I didn't know I'd never hear the end of it, I'd say good riddance." Tanner looped an arm around her shoulders and led her inside. Seeming to notice Keith wasn't following, he asked, "What are you waiting for, an engraved invitation?"

"You aren't seriously going to leave me here," Keith protested. Of course she was leaving him here or they wouldn't have driven into the middle of BFE otherwise. Still, he had to try, futile as the attempt was.

No longer hidden behind blackout shades, Marta's blue eyes glinted. "Once you've had his steaks, you won't want to leave."

He wasn't surrendering to her charm this time. "I know how this works. You have to set me up with appropriate work until I can find a job on my own. I don't see farmhand on my resume anywhere."

"You haven't seen your resume at all, Mr. Martin." Her charm had become something a bit frostier and a lot more implacable. "If it makes you more comfortable, Tanner needs a business manager, which you just might be qualified to do with your fancy MBA. And by having you way out here, it saves the Bureau a lot of money and man hours that can be better spent somewhere else. The farmhand work is a bonus."

"A bonus?"

"Like a gym membership." She winked.

Tanner grabbed Keith's duffel. "Don't worry. I'll take it easy on you. At first. You can start with the chickens and work your way up to the cows."

"I thought you said you had cowboys to handle that shit?" He had no choice but to follow them into the house.

"They handle the herds. I keep a flock of chickens, half a dozen dairy cows and some horses for my own use, as well as tending the garden."

"This is a nightmare."

"It might be, but you'll never eat better."

Keith had no choice but to go inside. He missed Houston, his apartment, his car, his friends, his life. He missed Ryan. But thanks to his father, all of that was gone now. He had nothing left but a farmhouse in the middle of Montana and the promise of an excruciating, embarrassing few months of menial labor. But, hey, he wouldn't be dead.

Thanks, Dad.

CHAPTER 2

Tanner tried not to judge people based on first impressions, but fifteen years in the service had taught him first impressions were rarely wrong. His first impression of Keith Martin was that the man going to be a pain in his ass from now until this thing with the Escavaras and his daddy was settled.

"The things you do for family," he grumbled, flipping over the steaks on the grill. Marta owed him big time for this. Big time.

Still, it could be worse. Keith wasn't the first of these marginally important "associated persons" the DOJ had needed to hide away for a few months. And he wasn't a criminal in his own right, meaning Tanner wouldn't have to keep watching his back and his stuff for the duration of Keith's stay. After the case was done, Keith would head off to greener pastures—Seattle, like he'd said, or maybe back East, leaving Tanner to his solitude once again.

"At least this one's pretty," Marta said from behind him, taking an innocent sip of her soda when he glared at her.

"Pretty doesn't get things done."

"Not always." She sidled up to him. "But it sure does improve the scenery, my dear cousin."

"Knock it off, Marta."

"So you can honestly say you don't find Keith the least bit attractive?"

He stabbed the steaks with more force than necessary as he plated them. "Are your bosses aware you keep trying to set me up with your pets?"

"Hell, no. You know the rules on fraternization."

"I lived with Don't Ask Don't Tell for three tours; I think I'm familiar with how it works."

"Well, give him a break. Keith's not a bad guy. He's just jet lagged and out of his element. He'll come around with a little patience."

"You might be right. But remember, do unto others. You don't have to live with him for the next three to four months." Then he asked, "Has it registered with him how long he is going to be here?"

"I think it's barely registered that he's staying overnight. Let him sleep in tomorrow, give him the tour, tell him his duties and then be a jackass to him the morning after."

"I have done this before, you know."

"I heard, Drill Sergeant. That's why I'm warning you off. This one didn't do anything wrong, so you've got no call to punish him."

"Where's the fun in that?" As soon as the words left his mouth, he regretted it.

Marta smirked. "Oh, this is going to be entertaining."

Ignoring her, he took the steaks into the kitchen and called out, "Food's on, city boy."

Keith came out of his room, and Tanner was startled by the transformation. His black hair was damp and now curled slightly at the ends, emphasizing eyes almost light enough to be gray. A fresh set of clothes set off his long, lean body to the best effect without looking like he was trying too hard. The shower seemed to have done wonders for his attitude as well. "It smells great. Is there anything I can do to help?"

"Tonight you're company. Marta, bring the man a beer."

"Oh, you did not just go there." But when she came out of the kitchen, she had three beers in one hand and a big salad balanced in the other.

"Hold on, aren't you still on-duty, Marshal?" Keith's voice had a teasing note to it, making him seem more human.

"I delivered you, checked in with my superiors, and am officially off-duty until tomorrow morning." She handed over a beer. "So you'd better be on your best behavior until after I leave."

"Yes, ma'am."

They all sat down at the table, and Tanner served up the steaks.

"Holy crap," Keith said with a touch of awe, "I thought we had big steaks in Texas."

"When you cut your own filet, you don't have to worry about how much it is a pound."

"And it's all grass fed." Marta knew the spiel as well as Tanner did by this point. "Tastes nothing like grain-fed. Go on, try it."

Looking skeptical, Keith cut a sizeable bite. His expression changed the moment he started chewing and the flavor registered. "What did you put on these? They're amazing!"

"Bit of salt and pepper; the rest is courtesy of the cow."

"Jesus..." Which was the last thing he said for quite some time.

Tanner made note for the future.

"So, a business manager, huh?" Keith finally initiated conversation, even though his mouth was half full.

"I'm good with the animals, not so much with the books," Tanner admitted. "I know enough to keep out of trouble with the IRS and get my bills paid, but it's hard to plan for future expansion. Think you can help?"

"Sure. But something tells me it won't get me out of farm work, will it?" Keith's eyes crinkled slightly, showing he wasn't completely serious.

Tanner opted to keep it light. "Hasn't got me out of it, yet."

"Who knows, I might surprise you."

"You won't understand the business if you don't do all of it."

"God, you're a hardass."

Marta interrupted before they could really get going. "You aren't telling him anything he doesn't already know. He's been like this since he was twelve. The only place for him to go was the military."

"What I don't get is how you go from military to"—Keith waved toward the seemingly endless expanse of land outside the picture window—"well, this."

"I got tired of not being my own boss," Tanner replied. Not to mention losing good friends to increasingly pointless wars.

As usual, Marta called him on his shit. "And nobody's shooting at you here." She turned to Keith. "I tried to convince him to join the Marshals Service, but he wasn't having it."

He glared at her and turned to Keith. "Fine. The real reason was I always wanted this and had enough saved up when I left the navy to finally do it."

"Now, was that so hard?" Marta said sweetly

"I can't imagine choosing this life."

Tanner bristled. "I've got cable and cell service, a T1 connection, a Jacuzzi and a big house with all the privacy I could want. There's nothing your city life can offer that I can't get here."

"Except company."

"I get plenty of company."

"Besides cowboys, marshals, and people like me?"

Marta surprised them both by shoving back from the table. "There's no point in fussing about it now, Keith. You're here until I take you out. Do you want another beer? I want another beer."

"Is she always this bossy, or is it just me?" Keith asked after she left.

"Always."

"Good to know."

Tanner relented. "Look, I get this isn't your scene. There are towns around, not the fancy kind you're used to, but they have bars so you can mingle. And Great Falls isn't too far…closer than Billings."

"But we still have to go over that godforsaken road of yours."

"Maybe you'll decide I'm not such bad company after all."

"If not, there's always Internet porn," Marta chimed in, as she returned with fresh bottles of beer.

"Stop helping," Tanner said.

She grinned. "Don't tell me you've become a prude after all these years."

"Keith and I have to live together. It'll be a lot easier without you introducing porn into the conversation."

"What possible other reason would a guy have a T1 connection and more than seven hundred cable channels out in the middle of God's country, if not for the porn?"

"Sports?" Keith suggested.

"See?" Tanner said.

She snorted into her beer. "Because most sports aren't a euphemism for porn anyway."

"Marta, with you, everything's a euphemism for porn."

"What's wrong with that?"

"Ignore my cousin," he said instead to Keith. "She was corrupted by being the only girl in a family full of boys."

Keith nearly choked on his beer. "Your cousin?"

"She didn't tell you?"

Keith shook his head.

Marta shrugged. "It never came up."

"Well, I hope you didn't hit on her. Since she doesn't have any brothers, it would fall on me to kick your ass."

"Have you seen her?" Keith looked incredulous. "If I did hit on her, I'm sure she could kick my ass fine on her own."

"And if I weren't used to the older brother schtick from Tanner, I'd be kicking his ass as well."

"Why didn't you tell me you were related?"

"Because it doesn't matter." She sipped at her beer, her expression still cool. "He's a contractor with the Service. You aren't here because he's my cousin; you're here because he volunteered to be a safe house."

"You don't have any cousins anywhere more civilized?"

"Billy's up in Alaska these days, isn't he?" Tanner tried not to smirk.

Marta gave Tanner an evil look. "Tracking whale populations off Baja."

"Wimp."

"And Billy isn't ex-navy. Tanner has a special skill set that makes him appropriate for these kinds of jobs, even if we weren't related. I'm not the only marshal who uses him." Her blue eyes danced as she continued, "It keeps him from getting too lonely out here in the middle of nowhere."

Keith's smile gave way to a yawn. "Sorry," he apologized.

"Don't," Tanner said. "Feel free to crash anytime. We don't stand much on ceremony around here."

"Yeah, I think I will." Rising, Keith took his plate and started to reach for the others.

"Leave 'em." Tanner took Keith's plate. "Tonight, you're still company."

"You sure?"

"Very. Marta's on dish duty anyway."

"In that case..." With a smile and a quick good night, Keith disappeared into his room.

When he was gone, Marta stood up and collected the abandoned dishes. "Well?"

"I don't know." Tanner followed her into the kitchen, carrying the empty salad bowl and beer bottles. "I'd expected him to be a lot more spoiled. There's some, but you can't blame a city boy. He seems to take it all in stride and then, out of the blue, balks. I'm not sure what to make of him."

"You certainly can't complain he's not easy on the eyes."

"Oh, he is. I'm sure all the ladies in Houston are missing him about now."

"He is quite popular with them."

Damn. He'd been kind of hoping— *No, not going there.* Tanner had scratched an itch or two with his charges in the past. The temporary nature of their stays allowed for the indulgence, despite the circumstances. But it was better when he didn't.

"Well, he'll be back with them sooner than he thinks," Tanner said finally.

"I doubt it." She began loading the dishwasher. "The Escaveras are pissed. Even if Lewis senior makes it to court, and if the court finds Amedeo Escavera guilty, the family's going to want revenge and to send a message there are consequences for ratting out the family, no matter who you are. Neither Keith nor his father will be going back to Texas in this lifetime. We'll be lucky if we can get them back in the same city together in the next two years."

Tanner rinsed and binned the bottles for recycling. "They close?"

"Enough. They're all each other has. No cousins or siblings."

"Wouldn't that be nice?"

Marta threw her dishtowel at his head. "I should make you finish cleaning up for that."

"Seeing as the dishwasher's already mostly loaded, I wouldn't consider it much of a hardship." Before she could throw something more damaging than a dishtowel at his head, Tanner picked up the recycling bin and ducked outside.

As he crunched across the drive to the shed where he kept trash and recyclables, his thoughts drifted back to Keith. Marta wasn't wrong. With his black hair, athletic build and soulful eyes, he was very easy to look at. But he didn't have the hard, defensive edge the other protected witnesses Tanner had sheltered had. Maybe that was why it had felt safe enough to sleep with them. Donny had been looking for some fun while he waited out his uncle's trial, and Quint had been so damn broken, sex with him had felt like the least Tanner could do.

But Keith was different. And Keith was straight. So Keith was off limits. Which promised some uncomfortable nights during the long, cold winter.

CHAPTER 3

It was disconcerting for Keith to wake up on his own without a call from some hotel receptionist or, worse, Marta leaning over the bed to shake him awake. It helped that the bed was big and comfortable and, for the first time in a month, he wasn't on the run for his life. And he thought he smelled coffee.

As homes away from home went, this one wasn't looking too bad.

Granted, he wasn't waking up next to Ryan. There had been some great mornings when the two of them had woken up and never gotten out of bed. But those days were gone now. One more victim of the Escaveras.

He pulled a robe on over his silk sleep pants and made his way down to the kitchen. For a log house, the place was remarkably modern, with high, airy ceilings and skylights to provide minimal interference with the vastness of the sky and land surrounding them. With heavy Craftsman furniture and thick carpets, the place had a strongly masculine feel to it, without being strictly utilitarian. It was the kind of place where you left your boots on the porch. Keith respected that.

There was a real, proper coffee maker in the well-appointed kitchen, not fancy enough to make cappuccinos, but good enough to brew a strong pot and keep it warm all day without burning it or making it taste like decomposing hydrocarbons. Keith poured himself a cup and went to look out the sliders onto the deck and the landscape beyond.

Keith had always considered Texas big. Every Texan did. But this endless emptiness was like nothing Keith had ever seen. He knew he could walk in a straight line for days and not see a road, a town, a house, even another living thing. And here he was, right in the middle of it. "Thanks again, Dad."

"I'll make sure to pass it along to him," a rough voice said behind him.

He turned to find Marta, perfectly dressed and ready for the day, save one small detail. Her eyes barely opened to half-mast.

"Coffee?" He tried not to smirk.

"Now. Before I find my gun."

Familiar with this reaction by now, he pressed his own mug into her hand and went to pour himself a fresh cup.

"Surprised you're up so early." She sank into a chair at the table.

"It's not really that early. I did have a day job, you know."

"After the past couple of weeks, I'd figured you'd want a sleep-in day."

He shrugged, taking a seat at the end of the table so he could talk to her without losing the view. "Just couldn't sleep, I guess."

"Oh, you'll be sleeping well enough once Tanner puts you to work."

Taking a long swallow of his coffee, Keith considered his next words. *Why the hell not?* "I don't like failure, and I have a feeling I'm going to be doing a lot of failing out here."

"So long as you make an effort, that's what counts." The caffeine seemed to be working its magic because he saw an all too familiar wicked glint in her more alert eyes. "It still doesn't mean you won't look like a prized ass the first time you milk a cow."

"Cow?"

She nodded. "He does six, all milked by hand. I've asked him to tape it."

"And after I was so nice to you." He reached for her mug.

Her grip on it tightened. "I've killed men for less."

"Don't think she's kidding," Tanner said from the front door, where he was pulling off a heavy pair of gloves.

Keith checked. No boots. Instead he'd slipped on a pair of rubber-soled driving mocs.

"I thought you were planning to put me to work."

"I am. I wanted to wait to give you the tour in daylight so you can find your way around, then you can help me with feeding time tonight."

He poured himself some coffee and joined them. "I think we may get snow tonight."

"You're kidding, right? It's only September!"

"Exit me, stage right, pronto." Marta took another sip and stood up. "I want to be off that goat path you call a road before it even starts thinking about snow."

Keith was about to protest when Tanner stood up to join her. "You sure you can't stay longer? Even if it's a heavy storm, you wouldn't be stuck here longer than a week this time of year."

She slung her duffel bag over her shoulder. "I'm sure. If I stay too long, the wrong people will start asking questions. Keith, you've got my number and the secure email account we set up for you. Get in touch any time, even if it's just to bitch about my cousin." She grabbed her cup off the table and headed for the door. "I'll try to get back up for Christmas."

"I want that mug back!"

She saluted Tanner with it before closing the door behind her.

They were both silent as they listened to her engine start and the Cherokee headed back down the long, winding two-track to the secondary road, which led to another secondary road until finally meandering its way back to the highway to Billings. Keith was overwhelmed with the sense of isolation.

"Didn't expect to see you up yet."

Tanner's voice startled Keith out of his thoughts. Grateful for the distraction, he didn't take offense. "Except on the weekends, I tend to be an early riser. Not as early as you're probably used to, but I'm not a fan of wasting the day."

"Not a lot of weekend out here. The cows don't really take any time off."

"Was she kidding about milking?"

"It's not so bad once you get used to it. It's a lot like—" He stopped himself, and Keith was surprised to see a slight flush in his high cheeks. "Never mind. But people make it seem a lot worse than it is. By the third day, you'll be an old pro."

Keith doubted it, but he was willing to try. "Marta was joking about the filming, right?"

"When it comes to humiliation, Marta doesn't joke. Much." Tanner smiled. "As for me, so long as you keep the bitching to a minimum, there's no need to record it for posterity."

"I appreciate that." Keith fingered the collar of his robe. "I guess I'd better go change so we can get this started."

"If you'd rather start off easy, I can show you the books and files. You don't have to jump right in."

Keith got up. "May as well get the worst of it over. It might make me actually look forward to paperwork."

"Nothing is as bad as paperwork."

"Which is why you need a business manager."

"Which is why I need a business manager."

Nodding, Keith finished off his coffee and stood. "I'll be out in five."

He didn't have a lot of choices for dressing, as all he had in the world at the moment were the clothes in the bag Marta had handed him when they started out on the roundabout trip out here. She'd known their ultimate destination, so instead of the slacks and dress shirts Keith normally wore in Houston, there were a couple of pairs of jeans, a few plain—thankfully—T-shirts, and some button-up shirts to wear over them. He dressed quickly and went back to the kitchen.

Tanner was cooking.

Keith couldn't decide which was more appealing at the moment— Tanner whistling as he moved around the kitchen with efficient ease, or the smell of fresh bacon frying.

"You keep pigs, too?" he asked.

"I tried." Tanner's gaze didn't quite meet his. "But it didn't work out."

There was a story there, but Keith didn't press, yet. They had a lot of time ahead of them.

"It's still locally grown, however," Tanner added. "Got a deal worked out with one of the other ranchers."

"How very...pioneering of you."

Tanner gave him a dirty look. "Do you want the bacon or not?"

"Oh, I most definitely do."

"Then you can drop the smart comments and set the table."

The tone he said it in was the same one he had used teasing Marta, and the half amused crinkle around his brown eyes confirmed he was using it the same way here, so Keith didn't take offense. "Sure thing, boss, right away!"

He finished setting the table just as Tanner wrapped up cooking. Bacon and eggs with toast, simple but surprisingly good. Coffee usually was about all the breakfast Keith went for. But out here...maybe it was something in the air.

17

They didn't talk much while they ate, which was just as well. Keith suspected they'd start to run out of topics of conversation pretty quickly. As soon as the food was gone, Tanner stood up. "Ready to see the place?"

"Ready as I'll ever be. I don't have any boots, though."

Tanner picked up both plates. "There are some extras over by the door. Find something that fits. And grab a hat and gloves, too. It's cold out there."

"Yes, Mom."

Tanner shrugged, loading up the dishwasher. "Or don't. Your choice."

"I have an aversion to cold, so I might as well see what I can find."

There was a pair of hiking boots that fit close enough to avoid blisters, sparing him, at least for now, from the ubiquitous choice of cowboy boots. Granted they were a practical and durable choice in an environment like this, but back in Houston too many in his circle had worn them as status symbols, and they carried with them the faint stink of wannabe cowboy, like wearing the boots made them more masculine somehow. It wasn't the boots that made a man masculine. Tanner was a prime example.

Keith stopped his train of thought cold. He had enough on his plate right now without throwing sex into the mix. He was still recovering from the loss of Ryan, and he was only going to be here a few months. From the conversation last night, he suspected Tanner might lean his way. All the more reason not to go there, especially out here in the middle of nowhere, where even casual probably wasn't casual in the end.

Finally dressed for the outdoors, he rejoined Tanner in the kitchen.

He was just finishing drying the last pan. "No boots in the house," he warned, glancing down.

"I figured, boss. Only wanted to make sure I met with your approval."

Tanner dried his hands, looking him over. Keith tried not to take it personally.

"Seems serviceable enough. We're going to have to take you into town for some decent gear of your own, though. You're going to be here a while."

"Don't remind me."

"Well, we'll have to distract you, then. And nothing beats work for distraction." After redressing in his outdoor gear, Tanner led the way outside.

It was colder out than the brilliant sky and bright sunshine promised. Keith's boots crunched on the gravel as they crossed the drive toward the barns. "The keys for all the cars are hanging up by the door," Tanner explained as they went. "You're welcome to use any of them you like, but for now, Marta doesn't want you going into town alone."

"I doubt I'd find my way there, let alone make it back."

"It's mostly a straight shot. Just a very, very long straight shot."

Tanner opened the gate into the barnyard, and for the first time, Keith realized the whole compound was fences within fences. Barbed wire led inward to split rail and then to this inner defense, a post and rail fence covered in chicken wire.

Tanner noticed him taking it in. "It keeps the smaller animals out. We get coyotes and a bear or two in this far occasionally, but this is mostly to keep my livestock in and the smaller stuff out."

"What do you do about the big stuff?"

"Scare it off, if I can. I've got some friends in land management who help out sometimes. Otherwise…" He shrugged.

Keith could live without seeing otherwise. Some people avoided cities because of crime. Keith avoided nature for its sheer unpredictability. At least in the city you knew where you shouldn't go if you wanted to avoid trouble. Out here, there was no such luck.

They stepped around the chickens scratching in the yard, who ignored Keith and Tanner with equal disinterest. One beautiful palomino, however, came up to the inner gate to greet them. Tanner smiled and reached out to scratch her nose. "Didn't you get enough before, you wanton hussy?"

She closed her eyes, not caring about his comment.

"This is Cally," Tanner introduced them, still rubbing her forelock. "She's my girl, aren't you, sweetheart?"

The horse whinnied and pushed her muzzle into Tanner's chest.

Keith reached out a hand, then dropped it.

"Go ahead, she doesn't bite."

"I wouldn't want to come between you and your girlfriend."

"Not a chance. She's a faithful one, aren't you, sweetheart?" The other horses, sensing a chance for treats, came over to check them out as well. Rather than open the gate, Tanner climbed the fence to join them. "Come on over. They won't bite."

"It's not their teeth I'm worried about." But Keith followed his lead, climbing the rails just off to the side of the clustered animals. They were too focused on Tanner to pay any attention to him.

"This is Clyde." Tanner slapped a tall bay on the withers affectionately. "He's got some years to him, but he's steady and reliable." He pulled a few broken carrot pieces out of his pocket. "Here. Make friends with him."

Clyde watched Keith with fathomless black eyes as he approached. Keith wasn't afraid, exactly, but he hadn't been this close to a horse since he was a teenager. "Christ, I forgot how big they could be."

Tanner chuckled. "This lot are lightweights compared to some."

"Wonderful." Keith held out the carrot to Clyde, who blinked at him. "What's he waiting for?"

"For you to get in reach, presumably. Go on. He's not going to step on you." Tanner gave him a shove, sending Keith nose to nose with the big horse. Clyde wickered with a shake of his head, then bent to take the carrot from Keith's hand. "Scratch his ears."

He did, surprised to find they were almost kitten-soft as opposed to the wiry coarseness of his dark mane. "Nice to meet you, Clyde. I guess you and I are going to be friends for the next few months."

Clyde shoved at his hand, looking for more carrots.

"Here." Tanner handed him a couple more. "Clyde's stomach leads him. Keep that happy and you'll never shake him."

He held one up for Clyde's greedy lips. "If only all guys were so easy to keep."

"They are, once you figure out what they like best." Before Keith could reply, Tanner moved on to the remaining three horses. He patted a gray, another palomino, and a horse that resembled a shaggy mutt, if such a thing were possible in the horse world. "This is Karen, Kenny, and Foster."

"What breed is Foster?"

"A mutt is my closest guess," Tanner echoed Keith's first impression. "I found him tangled up in one of my fences not long after I bought this place."

Keith scratched Foster's scruffy ears as well, earning an affectionate rub from the horse. "He's pretty friendly for a feral horse."

"I guess once he lost his herd and found a warm place with regular food, he figured he was better off. I let him run a lot, so he seems pretty happy."

Trailing his hand down Foster's neck, Keith looked at Tanner. "You take in a lot of strays, don't you?"

"Keeps things interesting." Tanner nodded toward the barn. "Now I've shown you the fun part, time to show you where the work is."

The barn itself was an enormous stone and wood structure fifty feet wide and nearly two hundred feet long. Tanner led them in through a door at the end. "It was the only thing standing when I looked at the place. I kept the herd in here winters when I started out, but now there's enough of them, they winter out in the pasture, and I use this mostly for hay storage."

Keith could smell the warm, damp musk of decomposing straw, but there were other, more mammal smells overlying it. "Mostly?"

"The horses are in here and the six milk cows. I also keep the two tractors, the harrow, reaper and bailer in here, as well as a couple of ATVs and snowmobiles for when the horses won't do."

"Right." Keith took it all in. "What's the routine around here?"

Tanner took him around, showing him where the feed and water was, where to get the fresh straw, where the chiller was for the fresh milk. Keith tried not to wrinkle his nose at the strong assault of smells, knowing it would just reinforce all Tanner's stereotypes about him.

"We'll have to milk the cows and feed everyone tonight, then tomorrow you can start helping with the real work."

"Well, I've always said I'll try anything once."

"And how's that worked for you?"

"I've had many pleasant surprises."

"Hopefully, this will be, too. You're lucky, really. The hardest work is over until spring. May and June I hardly ever see my bed."

"And you like this life?"

"Love it."

The genuine joy behind the words struck a chord with Keith. He'd enjoyed the life he'd had before well enough, but he honestly couldn't say he loved it.

"What next?" he prompted.

"Since I saw to the stalls earlier, we've got a few hours to kill until evening chores roll around. Which is when I attempt to do the paperwork portion of this operation."

"My kind of work."

"Sure you wouldn't rather go for a ride?"

"I think Clyde's had enough attention from me. I like to take things slow with a new relationship. And avoiding the paperwork is no way to grow your business."

"You haven't seen the paperwork." Tanner headed for the exit.

The other horses had wandered off while Keith and Tanner were in the barn, but to Keith's surprise, Foster still stood there, as though waiting for them. As soon as they came out, he ambled over to nudge at Keith's shoulder.

Tanner laughed. "Looks like you made a friend after all."

"Sorry, Foster, no more treats." Keith held up his empty hands.

Foster sniffed, then began to rub his nose against Keith's palm, not unlike a cat rubbing against your leg.

"I forgot to mention, Foster goes for petting like Clyde does for carrots."

Keith obliged. "Pretty odd for a wild born animal."

"He sure is. But he's family. Come on. Let's go look at the paperwork."

Keith gave Foster one last pat before following. Foster trailed along after them to the gate, watching them forlornly as they headed back to the house.

CHAPTER 4

When Tanner showed Keith into the den, Keith let out a low whistle. Tanner wasn't prone to exaggeration, much. At least it was in some semblance of order. Not the best, but better than not at all.

Paging quickly through a stack, Keith nodded to himself a few times. He looked up at Tanner, seriousness writ in his gaze. "I can tell you what your biggest issue is."

"No business sense." Tanner had made his peace with that fact long ago.

Keith shook his head. "No, you have plenty sense. Your problem is you're running it like it's twenty years ago. These days you don't need all of this paper." He fingered through some of the stacks. "How many years' worth is this?"

"A little more than seven."

"And you've owned the place how long?"

"Seven years."

"Man. Is any of this on the computer?"

Tanner was starting to feel like an antique. "Not much. The bank statements and income tax stuff are all online, but the invoices and receipts are all paper."

"All right, well, let me take a look at your—" Keith stopped with the chair half pulled out. "Tanner, how old is this computer?"

"Why, what's wrong with it?"

"It has a floppy disk drive."

"So? Some of my stuff's on floppies."

"You have a T1 connection and a computer too old to take advantage of it?"

"My laptop's newer. This is just for the business stuff."

"As your new business manager, I insist that your first business investment is going to be in a decent computer with relevant software. Christ, you're probably using Money, aren't you?"

"If it's what came with the computer, I did."

"Did?"

Tanner shrugged. "Never could get it to do what I wanted, so I gave up and have been using pen and paper." He pointed out the ledgers lining the bookshelf beside the desk.

"It didn't do what you wanted because it was a piece of shit from the get-go." Sighing, Keith finally sat and turned on the computer. "All right, while I'm busy dredging up decades' old computer knowledge, how about you get your laptop and start looking for something new?"

"Keith, I know cows, not computers."

Keith looked around. "You know what? You're probably right. Get me your laptop. I'll order it and then start getting this in some kind of order until the new machine comes. Christ, I may need a clerk to get all this data entry done."

"Keith—"

"Don't worry. I won't look at your porn stash."

"You won't be able to find it," Tanner said on his way out of the room. There was no point in fighting this. Keith was right. Tanner hadn't been investing the money back into the business the way he should have, focusing more on building the herd instead. It was time to put some of it into infrastructure.

Still, he wished Keith wouldn't mention porn quite so casually. It did erratic things to Tanner's libido.

This really would be so much easier if Keith was a pampered asshole like he was supposed to be. But no, he had to be halfway decent and willing to lend a hand.

"Thanks a lot, Marta," Tanner grumbled, retrieving his laptop from his bedroom and returning to the den.

"I can't believe you have Windows Me. No one ever used Me."

"Okay, you've made your point. I'm a hick. Get over it."

Keith took the laptop, then eyed it suspiciously. "This is running Vista, isn't it?"

"I can take it back." Tanner reached for it.

"No, you don't." Keith pulled it away protectively, then set it down on a bare space of desk and opened it. "If you want to help, you can move the coffee maker in here."

"No, I can't. But I can bring you a cup while you work."

Keith was already lost in what he was doing, waving approval to Tanner as he went to work.

As he was pouring the coffee, the humor of the situation struck him. "I'm like his damned secretary." Which gave him an idea.

"Here's the deal," he said when he returned. "If you can pull your weight with the farm work, I'll do the data entry."

Keith took the mug, looking dubious. "It's going to require a certain amount of speed and accuracy."

"I can learn. It's not like I don't get computers, I just don't care about them all that much. If I can handle setting up satellite uplinks in Kabul, I can type some numbers into a spreadsheet."

"You haven't done much data entry then." He smirked. "After several hours of inputting endless numbers into teeny boxes, you'll be longing for war zones."

"And you wouldn't rather face down the Escavaras than muck out those horse stalls?"

"Fair enough."

After about ten minutes of searching on the laptop, Keith turned it toward Tanner. "Here's the system you need."

Tanner studied the specs, though most of it was nonsense to him. "A terabyte? What the hell is that?"

"A shit-ton of memory. About a hundred times what you currently have on your old junker."

"But it's like a third of the price I spent on the last one."

"The wonders of technology, my friend."

Tanner looked at the price tag again. "It's still a lot of money. Couldn't we get something smaller?"

"Do you want to be buying another new computer three or four years down the line?"

"Not at that price."

"Trust me. This is what you want. Barring any truly astonishing breakthroughs in computer science, this will be upgradeable and adaptive for at least ten years. I promise you, you'll make the money back within a year with what we'll be able to do with it."

It pretty much killed the stipend he got for taking Keith in in the first place, but why the hell not? "Yeah, all right." He went and got his credit card and handed it over. "Here."

"You sure?"

"I hate those damned online forms. I haven't met a piece of hardware I can't handle. But software…yeah, better you do it."

Keith looked at the card. "This is your personal account, isn't it?"

"Yeah, why?"

"Because this is a business expense and should come out of your business account."

"It's all the same account."

Keith looked ready to have apoplexy.

"What?"

"I know what the next order of business is." Shaking his head, he started placing the order.

Tanner could hear him muttering under his breath the whole time.

Rather than suffer through it, he went out to the living room and collapsed on the sofa before picking up the phone.

Marta answered on the second ring. "I'll mail your mug back. Man, you're fastidious."

"That's not why I'm calling. Where are you?"

"I just turned onto Route 12. What's wrong? Do you need me to come back?"

"Maybe."

"Why? Did he hit on you?"

"Don't I wish." Shit, had he said that out loud? Hurriedly, he added, "That I could handle."

"His cover can't have been blown already."

"Not unless the Escaveras planted a spy among my horses."

"Last I checked, shifters were still a myth."

"Shifters? What? Never mind, I really don't want to know." Tanner sighed. "He's making me feel like an idiot."

"Oh, is that all?"

"It's more than enough. This is my business, my life, and he's in there telling me everything I'm doing wrong. And why would you think he'd hit on me?"

"Why wouldn't he hit on you?" she replied cagily.

"Marta, what the hell have you done?"

"Just my job, Tanner." He could almost see the impish smirk when she added, "And maybe given you the chance to broaden your horizons."

"Damn it, Marta." He practically growled the words.

"You usually have the case files memorized beforehand. Don't blame me for you not realizing it sooner."

"How in the hell do I get gay from a guy who's essentially the playboy of Houston with all the eligible women?"

"Fine print, Tanner, fine print."

"What fine print?"

"All the mothers love him. He's always a gentleman and never goes out with the same girl more than twice. Because on the third date he'd be expected to at least kiss her. He's not in the closet. I asked him. He just keeps things very quiet. And you've got a whole lot of quiet."

"Thanks a lot."

"It's never been an issue for you before. And Keith's better than the other ones you've slept with in the past."

"I don't like being set up, Marta."

"Yes, because I went out of my way to get his daddy in trouble with a Mexican drug cartel just to get you a date. He's a good guy, Tanner. He had a boyfriend back in Houston who he had to leave behind and won't ever see again, and he needs someplace to be safe and feel useful. And you need to not be so goddamn alone all the time."

Marta always was sticking her nose in where it didn't belong. "I like my life fine as it is, so butt out."

"Sure you do," she said. "Just try not to take out your anger at me on him. All right?"

"You told him about me?"

"It never came up."

"Goddamn it, Marta—"

"I didn't want him thinking I was delivering him up there as a houseboy, Tanner. Besides, now you get all the fun of seeing how long it takes for him to realize you're coming on to him."

"I'm not going to come on to him."

"Bet ya."

"No."

"Three days, tops. How long's it been for you anyway, Tanner? At least a couple months, right?"

"None of your business."

"It's been my business since we were thirteen and you first started figuring this out. You've told me just about every encounter you've ever had, including the reporter who was embedded with you in Afghanistan. I know what attracts you and I know what gets you off. No, I didn't set you up with Keith, but he's just the kind of guy I'd pick for you if I was looking." Finally she took a breath. "So grow the fuck up and talk to him. Or don't talk. Not talking is pretty good, too, if it's done the right way."

"I'm hanging up now, Marta."

"Coward," she managed to get through before he broke the connection.

Great. Now what was he going to do?

He probably should have picked something up sooner. But he hadn't been looking for it, seeing Keith more as a victim or as a greenhorn who was going to need hand-holding. Suddenly the conversation out in the corral took on much more meaning, something he hadn't even paid attention to at the time.

"Damn it."

"Everything okay?"

Tanner didn't jump or blush or give any other foolish response, but only thanks to years of practice. He really hoped Keith hadn't been standing there long. "Just checking in with Marta. You know how family can be."

"No, not really."

"Ah, right. She said you just had your dad." He glared at the phone. "I could envy that."

"It has its ups and downs, same as anything." Keith handed back Tanner's credit card. Tanner ignored the small spark when their fingers brushed. "I'm going to grab a shower now, then we're going to talk about the benefits of incorporation and separation of assets."

"Sounds exciting."

"Oh, believe me, it's not. Have plenty of coffee waiting when I get out."

"Can't wait." He tried not to watch Keith walk out of the room. *Damn Marta and her damned suggestions.*

He could empty the dishwasher in addition to making fresh coffee. That should kill all of two minutes. Hopefully, Keith showered fast.

CHAPTER 5

The snow Tanner had predicted started overnight, waking Keith from a sound sleep with a howl of wind that shook the house when it hit. The two of them trudged through snow, already up around their ankles, to do the morning chores. Thankfully, the barn was warm enough and sheltered from the wind, but neither of them said much aside from Tanner's succinct directions while they worked. He seemed to be more from the learn-by-doing school of teaching, so he shoved a milk machine in Keith's hands and demonstrated how to latch it on. Keith was relieved he wasn't going to have to do it manually, although he suspected it was only the storm keeping Tanner from making him have a go at it.

"What do you do with the milk?" Keith asked, watching the thin white liquid travel through the tubes into collection buckets.

"Drink some of it. The rest I keep for a local cheese maker. She comes around every three or four days to collect it."

"Does it pay well?"

"Well enough. And I get some of the cheese, which makes it worth it."

Tanner walked him through the sterilization process once they were done and then both of them took up pitchforks and shovels to muck out the stalls. Having been kicked out while Tanner and Keith cleaned, the horses huddled woefully around the stable door, snow clinging to their backs and getting trapped in their manes, despite how often they twitched their necks in a vain attempt to dislodge it. Tanner finished first, leaving the odd stall out for Keith, while he put out food and fresh water for cattle and horses alike. As soon as Keith opened the stable door, the horses all trotted in gratefully, Foster pausing only to push at Keith with his head before finding his way to his stall.

"I think they have the right idea," Tanner observed. "Let's get back inside."

Tanner kept a fire going all day and lots of coffee made, but Keith kept eyeing the snow building up on the deck warily. "Is it always like this?" he asked, taking a break from database construction on Tanner's laptop to stand at the sliding doors, watching the endless haze of white obliterate all shape and color from the land outside.

Tanner looked up from the leather he was reconditioning. "No. This is early. Don't worry, though, a lot of it will blow away over the next few days."

"But not for long."

Tanner shook his head. "Come December, that's pretty much what it's going to look like. There will be a few gorgeous blue sky days, though, that will take your breath away."

"You're a glass half-full kind of guy, aren't you?"

Tanner grinned and went back to his work.

They did chores together again in the evening, except this time Tanner let Keith lead, correcting any missteps with gruff but non-judgmental patience. Still, by the time they were done, Keith was exhausted and hurt all over.

A hot shower and a handful of ibuprofen didn't do much to ease the well-earned muscle aches, and Keith found himself tossing and turning until nearly midnight. He sat up and looked at the clock. Ryan would still be out at the clubs. It was tempting to call and hear his soft tenor for the first time in weeks. The Escaveras hadn't known about him, so he was safe, but Marta had warned Keith not to make contact. Everything about his old life was gone now, even his lover. But there wasn't anything to replace it with. The deep silence around the house reminded him how isolated and empty he was. It wasn't a good feeling.

Finally, he surrendered and got up to raid the kitchen.

The house was dark, but to his surprise, the deck was lit by a blue glow reminiscent of a UFO landing that bled in through the sliding windows to tint the kitchen and living room. The snow had let up, now drifting down in gentle, easy flakes to recover the areas of the deck that had been shoveled clean, leading to a square Jacuzzi. Tanner relaxed in it, a beer nestled in a mound of snow kept nearby for the purpose, flakes scattered over his hair like confetti. He didn't notice Keith until he opened the sliding door.

"You've been holding out on me."

"Sorry. This is how I always celebrate the first snowfall of the year."

"You can take the SEAL out of the water, but not the water out of the SEAL, huh?"

"Something like that. You can come in if you want. There's plenty of room."

The thought of being outside and wet when it was still so bitterly cold was beyond common sense to Keith. "No, I don't think so."

"Oh, come on. The water's almost ninety. You won't freeze."

"Until I get out."

"You're three steps from the door. You'll be fine. Get in."

"I don't have a swim suit."

"Keith, you're in the middle of fifteen hundred acres of nothing but cows and snow. If you're that modest, wear your tighty-whities."

He didn't want to admit he slept in the nude, and the realization Tanner was probably naked under the water as well made the situation even more problematic. Still, there was something daring about joining him that appealed to Keith.

Tanner seemed to sense his surrender. "Leave your robe on the kitchen chair so it's warm when you get out."

Taking a mental breath, Keith shed the robe and stepped out onto the deck.

His arousal was instantly no longer an issue. "Holy shit!"

"Get in!" Tanner laughed before Keith could bolt back inside. "You'll be fine in a minute."

Keith didn't hesitate, stepping down into the pool without bothering to check the temperature. The warmth of it enfolded him as he sank into the water up to his neck. The delicious counterpoint of heat and cold was instantly both relaxing and invigorating, and Keith found himself sinking lower, resting his head against the side of the tub, his eyes closing in bliss.

"Good, isn't it? It was my one big splurge when I built the place."

"As if buying a ranch in Montana isn't a splurge."

Tanner shrugged. "I had a lot of money when I got out of the service. Had to spend it somewhere."

"Somewhere cold?"

"Somewhere not the desert."

"One harsh climate to another, then?"

"I like a challenge." Tanner slipped lower in the tub. "And there's more life out here."

"No IEDs, just cow pies."

"Yeah."

Keith was relaxed enough now that awareness of their mutual nudity was starting to reassert itself. He slouched farther into the water, trying not to think about it. "Well, if you had to get away from it all, at least you brought all the right things with you."

"I like my creature comforts."

"Indoor plumbing is a comfort. Jacuzzi is a bonus."

"Hard work deserves some kind of reward, don't you think?"

"After today I do. My God, I hurt."

"The hot water will help. But make sure you stretch good in the morning. In a few days, you won't even notice it." Tanner looked thoughtful for a minute. "Although, if we go riding tomorrow, I'd better heat the tub up for you again. You'll need it."

Keith cringed. "How much riding?"

"All day."

"I thought torture was illegal."

Tanner studied him with those dark chocolate eyes of his, and Keith knew he was being tested. "You don't have to come."

It would be easy and probably incredibly smart for him to take the out. But somehow, he didn't think Tanner would like it if he did. "No, I'll come. I'll just get even by bitching the whole way."

Tanner seemed happy with the response, as he settled a little deeper in the water. "You know, you're going to get the same chance I did soon."

"Chance?"

"New start. New life. Have you given any thought to who you want to be when you get out of here?"

"It still hasn't sunk in that I won't be going home after this." He brushed aside another thought of Ryan, who was probably already getting on with his own life without Keith. "I'd be lying if I didn't say the fresh start didn't hold some appeal. Finally out from under Dad's shadow and no longer having to play the stupid social games in Houston."

"Really? From what I read, it seemed like you enjoyed that scene."

"I did. Parts of it anyway. I like people. But you can never really be yourself in such an environment, if that makes any sense. It's like swimming with sharks. They're fine until you cut yourself."

"And did you?"

"I came pretty close. Fortunately, the other person had as much to lose as I did." Keith shook his head. "Never get involved with siblings."

"I thought you didn't have any siblings."

"Not my siblings... Never mind. Like you said, it's the past now. No point in worrying about it."

Tanner watched him intently for a moment, then shrugged. "Suit yourself."

Keith waited. "Aren't you even curious?"

"Of course I am, but it's still none of my business."

"We're stuck in a house together for the next few months. I would imagine in that time there won't be a lot that's not your business."

Tanner picked up his beer again. "You'll tell me if you want me to know."

Keith didn't know why he was so irritated. Actually, he did know. He wanted Tanner to get it, wanted him to read him and know he was attracted and, well... Suddenly, the whole situation seemed like a really bad idea.

Keith shoved himself out of the tub, ignoring the slap of below zero air against his hot skin. "I should get back to bed."

"Most people are happy to have others mind their own business."

"I'm fine," Keith insisted.

And then he remembered his erection.

His body was still warm enough from the water that the cold air hadn't had its usual effect, leaving him half erect and exposed. Tanner obviously noticed, but only took a sip of his beer as he met Keith's eyes.

There was no real way to protect his dignity, so Keith just turned and stalked into the kitchen, grabbing his robe as he passed.

In the safety of his room, he sank down on the bed in mortification and guilt. Leave it to him to be attracted to his keeper. Nothing like a little Stockholm syndrome to make his protective custody complete. Tanner was probably out there laughing at him.

Keith had the phone in his hand, Ryan's number half dialed before he realized it. He dropped the phone back on the bedside table, staring at it until it went dark in sleep mode again. All he wanted right now was someone to talk to, but the only person for fifty miles was the one person he most needed to talk about.

In that moment, he hated his father, the Escaveras, Marta and Tanner all equally.

CHAPTER 6

Tanner watched Keith go, admiring the flex of his ass as he stormed off.

It wasn't fair of him to keep quiet, and part of him felt like a heel. But he also knew if and when Keith felt comfortable enough to tell him, then maybe it would be appropriate to make a move on him. Right now he was lost and adrift, and Tanner would be damned if he was going to be some flotsam for Keith to hang onto. Keith had to sink or swim on his own. It was too early to tell which was more likely.

Which didn't keep Tanner from finding him far too attractive.

Now, alone with nothing to distract him from his own thoughts but the beer and the gentle hum of the Jacuzzi, he let himself wonder. A temporary indulgence. Nothing more.

Damn, he wanted Keith on his knees. The man had a gorgeous mouth, and Tanner was definitely curious about how it would feel around his cock.

But getting him there was where the mystery lay.

Would Keith need a slow seduction or a brazen offer? Did he need to be teased and tempted, or did he prefer to be commanded?

Or would he take the initiative?

There was no telling, and frankly, all prospects appealed to Tanner.

He watched the clouds blowing past over the full moon overhead, but didn't really see them. Instead, he was remembering Keith, the subtle proportions of his body, the dark hair making a line down his firm abdomen to an equally well-proportioned cock. Screw Keith on his knees. Tanner wanted a taste of that.

Taking another swallow of beer, he set the bottle aside and, instead, took hold of his own dick. If he was going to do this, then he was going to do it right. There wasn't any chance of him being interrupted now, not when Keith was too embarrassed to come out of his room.

Tanner kept his strokes languid as he composed the scene.

The current setting was just about perfect. Keith had looked good in the water, the refraction and light hiding his more salient features from Tanner's gaze, but emphasizing the sculpted muscles of his chest and shoulders, the snow contrasting with his black hair. If Tanner had slid over, it would have been so easy to lean close and tease at those full lips.

Ready for bed, he would have recently brushed his teeth, mouth tasting of lingering traces of mint. Fresh. And pliant.

Just the thought of kissing him was more erotic than it should be. Tanner could almost feel their bodies bobbing together in the water, the only contact accidental, except for his mouth on Keith's and his hand cupping Keith's head.

A hand, still mostly smooth, save for the faint calluses beginning to form, would wrap around Tanner's cock. It would be sure, not hesitant. Keith was no novice. His grip would be firm as he got acquainted with what Tanner liked.

Tanner would take the time to caress down Keith's chest, the water closing around his fingers as he followed the trail he had admired down between Keith's legs. He could almost hear Keith's soft groan as Tanner took hold of his cock as well.

Then Tanner realized he was hearing himself, groaning to the sky as he stroked himself under the warm water.

The thin layer of water easing his movements added just enough disconnect he could pretend the hand on his dick wasn't his own.

It would be so easy to let the buoyancy of the water lift him to straddle Keith's leg, pinning him to the side of the tub as he took both their cocks in hand. Even as he deepened their kiss, he would rock against Keith's body, balls and chest caressing through the water as Keith dug his fingers into Tanner's ass, encouraging every motion.

"Fuck me," Keith would say when mere contact wasn't enough.

Tanner would promise, "Next time," as he worked to bring them both off.

Keith would gasp, his handsome face even more sensual when lost in orgasm. Tanner could feel the jolts along Keith's cock as he came before realizing it wasn't his fantasy at all, but his own cock, his own orgasm as he jerked himself to completion.

Christ, why hadn't he moved on Keith while he was here?

Because it was only two days into this arrangement and there was a very long winter ahead. Too soon to fuck things up. Far too soon.

He reached for his beer again, watching the clouds part to reveal an endless sea of stars. If Keith didn't figure things out soon, it was going to be a *very* long winter.

CHAPTER 7

The next morning, while they were mucking out the stalls, Tanner broke the bad news. "I know I promised you a trip into town, but we're going to have to put it off until tomorrow." He levered another load of matted straw into the oversized wheelbarrow. "After that storm, I need to ride farther than I was expecting, over to the lower fences to make sure nothing came down."

Keith tamped down his disappointment. He was already starting to feel the walls of the house closing in around them, and he'd been looking forward to a pair of boots that actually fit. "I understand. Do you still want me to come along?"

"Only if you want to. It's likely to be a long day."

"I want to. If I stay in the house any longer, I'll scream."

Tanner forked over another load and grinned. "You get used to it. You just don't have enough to keep you busy yet. By the time the snow really flies, there'll be more to distract you."

Keith wished one of those distractions wasn't Tanner's mouth.

After they finished with the stalls, they went in to change before riding out. "You can't wear clothes you've been sweating in out in this weather," Tanner instructed. "Even though it's likely to get in the low forties today, the wind'll eat right through you and chill you right down if you're damp. Change into some long johns and layers. There's extra in the dresser if you need them."

Long johns? He really was in a different world out here. But Keith went in to change without protest. Complaining wouldn't change anything anyway.

He added an extra pair of heavy socks to the thermal wear under his jeans, and layered a T-shirt, flannel work shirt and a heavy sweater on top. It wasn't quite mummifying, but he could definitely feel his movement restricted.

Tanner was pulling heavy leather work gloves over wool liners when Keith came out. To Keith's surprise, he still only had on the barn coat he'd been wearing for chores earlier, although presumably he wore layers similar to Keith underneath. "Don't you have anoraks for this kind of work?"

"They're too bulky." Tanner wrapped a black woolen scarf around his neck, tucking the ends into his coat. "If we have to fix any wire, the barbs would eat right through rip-stop nylon. You'll be warm enough once we get riding."

Keith wasn't sure what made him more nervous, the cold or riding.

It appeared Tanner had been busy while Keith was getting ready. Cally and Clyde were saddled and waiting for them at the gate, Foster nosing about as if trying to figure out where they were going all decked out.

Tanner shoved Foster away gently, but the horse looked at him as though he'd hit him with a stick, hurt and sulky. Keith stopped to rub his ears. "Don't worry, boy. Maybe next time."

Foster pressed his forelock against Keith's shoulder, for all the world as though he were showing affection. Then, with a last snuffle, he turned and shambled off to join the others in the corral.

"Damnedest thing I've ever seen," Tanner said, already mounted on Cally. "You sure you're not a secret horse whisperer or something?"

"Well, I can whisper, but I doubt they're listening." He eyed Clyde uncertainly before fitting his foot in the stirrup.

Clyde seemed to sense Keith's unease and didn't move until Keith had steadied himself between the ground and saddle. "I thought fear was supposed to spook horses," he said, as he willed himself not to panic when Clyde took a few steps forward.

"Not Clyde. That's why he gets all the first-timers." Tanner grinned. "Then again, he might just be lulling you into a false sense of security."

Keith nearly stumbled as he swung himself up into the saddle. Clyde didn't move. "You think you're so funny."

"Yeah, I do. Come on. There's a lot of fence to ride."

If he weren't so focused on not breaking his neck, he would have been able to come up with a witty retort. Maybe.

Tanner led the way out of the corral and across the drive, headed away from the mountains and in the general direction of the main road. He pulled up at a metal gate in the long line of barbed wire and leaned down to pull up the latch to let it swing open, gesturing for Keith to go through. Once he had, Tanner followed him and pushed the gate closed again and latched it. "None of the main herd is in these pastures, but I let the milk cows out here occasionally, so it's best to make sure there's nowhere they can sneak out. Finding them when they get out is a bitch."

"They don't just come home for milking?"

"They will, if they haven't fallen in a ravine and broken their necks or gotten chased down by wolves."

"And you chose this life."

"I did." He pulled ahead of Keith, following the fence away from the drive along the line of the barn. "I'm used to things lying in wait to kill me. Out here, I'm the only one with a gun."

In all this desolation, the thought wasn't as reassuring as it should be.

They didn't talk much as they rode. The wind, while not fierce, was cold enough to pull at their breaths, making it the wiser choice to keep their mouths shut and their eyes open. Or at least that's how it seemed to Keith. Pasture after pasture, they rode through drifting snow whispering through half-buried skeletons of the summer's grass. Every once in a while, Tanner would stop and dismount, pulling out a heavy staple gun to tack a broken length of wire into place. Occasionally Keith had to get down as well, and between the two of them, they would wrestle a new stretch of wire out of its coil into a straight line between two fence posts like some wickedly barbed snake. As the day wore on, mounting was becoming more automatic for Keith. Or maybe he was just too cold and tired to worry about it anymore.

The sun was sinking well toward the horizon by the time Tanner said, "We're done out here. Let's head back."

"Done?" Keith honestly didn't believe him. The fence was never-ending, and he'd forgotten there was such a thing as warm.

"It'll be dark soon, and the moon won't be up for hours. Even following the road, we don't want to be out when we can't see what's in front of us."

Keith hadn't noticed the rough two-track just the other side of the fence; the drive Marta had brought him out what seemed like a lifetime ago. He followed Tanner obediently through the next gate they came across. Clyde seemed to know where they were headed and perked up, his gait a little quicker than Keith had gotten used to.

"We're well past their dinner time, so that should help motivate them," Tanner called back.

Still, it was almost pitch black by the time they sighted the exterior lights on the barn, lit automatically by the sensors attached to them.

Keith groaned when they dismounted, and even Tanner seemed grateful to be out of the saddle finally. "You were a big help today," he said, gathering up the reins of both horses. "Thank you."

"I think I'm crippled."

Tanner laughed. "Come on. You can feed the critters while I brush these two down."

As long as Keith kept moving, he knew he would be fine. So he went to tend to the animals. He had never missed city life more.

He had just finished putting out fresh straw for the horses when Tanner came up with a basket of eggs and a note. "You're in for a treat. Cecily was here."

"Who's Cecily?"

"The cheese maker I told you about." He gestured with the note. "She came by to pick up what was in the chiller and left us some goodies in the fridge inside."

"You leave your house unlocked so anyone can walk in?"

Tanner gave him a dirty look. "You worried a bear's going to get in and steal the TV?"

"No."

"All right then. She also says"—he gestured again with the note—"Margaret, the postmistress in town, has a couple of packages for me. I'm betting it's the new computer."

That actually did cheer Keith up. "Now you'll see how much easier your finances will be to manage with the right tools. From this century."

"Yeah, well." Maybe he was wrong, but he thought Tanner smiled ever so briefly. "If the weather holds, we'll head into town first thing. Then you can work your magic."

Keith took a step toward the house and winced. "If I can still move tomorrow."

"You're welcome to the hot tub. I'll even let you have it to yourself."

"No, that's not fair to you," he said. "About last night, I didn't—"

Tanner waved him off. "There's nothing to worry about and it's plenty fair. I'm actually used to this work. Go on." Tanner gave him a shove toward the house. "You have a soak while I make dinner. I'll even dig out my bathing suit for you."

Keith hurt too much to argue.

CHAPTER 8

It was hard to stay true to his word and leave Keith in peace in the hot tub, but Tanner had never been one for whipping a hurt animal, so he concentrated on making dinner and kept his back to the sliding doors. When the meal was ready, he tapped on the glass and made eating motions. Keith nodded and dragged himself out of the tub, apparently too tired to care about modesty, his robe clutched in one hand, only Tanner's bathing suit covering him as he went to get dressed. Tanner shook his head as he pulled out glasses to set the table. At this rate, putting on that suit was probably the closest he was going to get to Keith's cock.

Keith continued to be quiet through dinner until Tanner really started to get worried. "Are you okay?"

Keith waved him off, still poking at his salad. "I'm fine. Just bone tired."

"There's a game on tonight if you want."

"Yeah, okay." His interest wasn't feigned, but distant, unfocused.

Keith helped clear the dishes until Tanner sent him to the couch out of pity. "You'll get used to it. You worked your ass off today. You're allowed to be tired."

"You aren't."

"Like I said before, come spring, I don't sleep for weeks at a time. Go sit down. You can cook tomorrow to make up for it."

By the time Tanner finished up and grabbed two beers out of the fridge, Keith was already sound asleep on the couch.

Tanner watched him for a few minutes, shamelessly taking advantage of Keith's vulnerable state. Then, with a sigh, he set down the beers and pulled an afghan over his houseguest. "I didn't really care about the game, anyway."

*   *   *

Keith didn't wait for dinner to make it up to him. When Tanner got up at six-thirty the next morning, Keith was already up and concentrating on making omelets with the leftover bacon and some of Cecily's butterkase cheese.

"Smells fantastic," Tanner said as he entered the kitchen.

Keith grinned back at him. "It's the bacon. Makes up for a multitude of sins."

"Don't sell yourself short." Tanner stole a piece of cheese off the cutting board. "Although, I'm giving Cecily credit, too."

"As you should," Keith agreed, then turned back to the stove. "I've missed cooking. Didn't do it much before, but not having done it at all the last few months…yeah, it's good."

"It can't have been easy, giving up your old life." Tanner pulled out plates and glasses and poured orange juice while they talked.

"Some of it was easier to give up than others." Keith shrugged. "Hell, part of me welcomes the change, getting away from the games."

"This place has a way of doing that to you."

Keith looked puzzled when he turned to slide the omelet out onto a plate.

"You're closer to the edge here. It helps you see what's really important."

"Weren't you on the edge in Afghanistan?"

"I was practically over the edge there. Doesn't let you see much of anything except the gun in your hand."

"I can imagine." He grimaced. "No, I can't. I hate when people pretend to understand something they can't. Sorry."

"Don't worry about it."

Keith had already turned away to pull a second omelet out of the oven where he had kept it warm. He slid this onto the second plate and sat down at the island to eat. "So what's the plan today?"

Tanner picked up his own fork. "Once we get everyone fed and milked and all, we need to take the truck and go into town."

Keith perked up again. "That's right. I'd forgotten about the

44

computer."

"Among other things. We need groceries, especially if the snow's already starting, and you need some decent clothes of your own. I also need to get feed for the cows, so we'll take the truck."

"You don't have it delivered?"

"The feed?"

"The feed and anything else you use around here. Buy in bulk; have it delivered. Saves money and time."

"I prefer to buy local."

"No one locally sells in bulk?"

"That's not the way it works, Keith. All the growers around here sell to the feed mill, and the mill sells to the ranchers. And you may not have noticed, but the nearest big box store is six hours away."

"Makes sense, at least in good will, if not business-wise."

"This isn't the big city. People work differently. They take time, and they take care of each other." He hoped he hadn't loaded that statement up too much.

"True. In the city, everyone's looking out for themselves, so get out of the way." Keith stabbed at his omelet. "And I was one of them—am one of them. Doesn't matter."

"You go along to get along."

"Yeah, well, look where it got me."

"This isn't your fault. Your father was the one in bed with the Escaveras."

"Yeah, but I didn't try to stop him."

"Did you know about it?"

"I didn't not know, if that makes any sense. I never saw them in his offices or anything, but they were always around somehow in a distant orbit around Dad. I never even asked."

"Probably better you didn't."

"Maybe. And it's not as if Dad would have listened if I'd tried to talk sense into him."

"Sounds like it's a good thing you're here, then. We've got a whole lot of what you need."

"What?"

"Perspective." Tanner wiped his mouth and got up from the stool. "Come on. Sooner we get to chores, sooner we can head out. It's a long drive into town."

*   *   *

There was a light dusting of snow in miniature drifts alongside the road as they headed into town, hinting at the winter to come. Keith looked out the window, not in depression or disinterest, but actually looking around at the countryside. "How do you get out when it snows?"

"I have plows for the truck and one of the tractors. If it gets really bad, there are snowmobiles."

"You can ride snowmobiles into town?"

"Yeah, but your teeth don't stop rattling for about an hour after you get there."

"Then you need better snowmobiles."

Tanner grinned. "How do you know I didn't mean the cold?"

"Because I may be a city boy, but I've done more than ski on snow. Wear the right gear and the cold barely touches you."

"Sure, if you're out goofing around making an impression on the trails in Aspen. Try doing what we did yesterday on the back of a snow machine and see how you're feeling afterward."

Keith suddenly looked a little white around the eyes.

"And machines don't give off body heat."

"All right, you have a point."

Tanner pulled up at the end of the access road to lock the gate behind them and check the mailbox. Bills, the mortgage, junk mail, the usual. He climbed back into the truck and handed the bills to Keith. "There you go, business manager."

Keith looked through them. "Hey, so long as we're paying for it with your money, I'm good."

As they pulled out onto the blacktop, Tanner asked, "Speaking of money, have you got the cash stipend Marta gave you?"

"In my wallet. Why?"

"Because I'm going to drop you off at Weaver's to pick out some clothes, while I go get the feed. Unless you want me there to tell you if your new jeans make your ass look big."

The faintest of blushes tinged his high cheekbones, but he responded easily, "I think I can manage. That's what mirrors are for, right?"

"I always thought so." Tanner wouldn't let himself be disappointed by Keith's answer. "Do you need a list of what to get?"

Keith glared at him. "I think I can manage, Mother."

"Don't blame me if you freeze your ass off." And what a shame that would be.

They rode the rest of the way in silence.

CHAPTER 9

Weaver's was a hardware store. Keith knew it because the sign over the door said so. "I thought I was getting clothes."

"You are." Once again, Tanner seemed amused by his confusion.

"It's a hardware store," Keith stated, as though talking to an idiot.

"Just relax and get out of the truck."

Clothes at a hardware store. God, he *was* out in the sticks. But he did need something, so he got out.

"Should be back in an hour," Tanner called after him.

Keith slammed the door and stalked off. Clothes from a hardware store, and it was supposed to take him an hour?

A bell chimed as he entered the store. Not an electronic one, but a real, tiny, dangly bell. Maybe he'd stepped back in time as well.

"Well, well, look what the cat dragged in," a blonde behind the cash register greeted him. "You must be Tanner's latest."

He'd heard small towns were like this, everyone knowing everyone else's business. "I'm Keith. Keith Martin." His new last name still came so awkwardly. At least he didn't fumble over it like he first had— hours of practice with Marta had seen to that.

"Chrissy Walters. What can I get for you, Keith Martin?"

He looked around at the hardware and fishing tackle doubtfully. "Clothes mostly. I need a field coat and some boots—"

"Stop right there. That's all Pop's department. You head on back and up the stairs on the left and you'll find everything you need."

"Pop's department?"

"What? You think just because I'm a girl I should be dealing in clothes?" She grinned. "Sweetie, trust me. You don't want me anywhere near dressing you." Her eyes trailed over him. "Though, I wouldn't mind trying."

As out of his element as he was, he didn't feel enough up to his old flirt to play games. "On the left, you said?"

"Oh, well, couldn't hurt to try. We don't get a lot of new meat through here. Yup, go on up. I'll let him know you're coming."

A man bearing a passing resemblance to Sam Elliott greeted him upstairs. "Don't mind Chrissy; she's mostly harmless."

"I can still hear you, Pop!"

"Worse than her mother." He held out his hand to Keith. "Derek Walters."

"Keith Martin. I have to ask, who's the Weaver in Weaver's Hardware?"

"My wife's family, Chrissy's grandmother. There weren't any Weavers left who wanted the business, so she got it. It's just Chrissy and me now. So you're looking to get outfitted?"

"I'm not sure what I need, just that it should be warm and fit."

"You came to the right place then."

He'd come to the only place, as far as he could tell. But Keith refrained from comment and did his best to be personable. It wasn't Derek's fault Keith was in this situation.

"Are you working the ranch with Tanner or just staying at the house?"

He hadn't realized it was an option. "Definitely working."

"All right, then, let's set you up."

Inside of fifteen minutes, Keith was piled up with flannel-lined jeans, heavyweight shirts, wool socks, a waterproof duck cloth quilted snowsuit, an equally warm but surprisingly light field coat and a pair of chocolate brown round toed cowboy boots, all without trying on anything but the boots.

"I wouldn't be very good at my job if I couldn't tell your sizes by looking at you," Derek replied when Keith said as much. Then he added three pairs of gloves, two hats and a scarf to the pile. "Anything else?"

"Yeah. What do you wear in the summer?"

Derek didn't miss a beat. "Son, this is for summer."

Keith couldn't help snorting. "Does everyone out here have a witty sense of humor?"

"It's how we survive. You'll get used to it."

"Looking forward to it." He pulled out his wallet. "How much do I owe you?"

Derek waved him off. "I'll put it on Tanner's bill. Figure it's the least he owes you for putting you to work this time of year."

What the hell else was he supposed to spend money on in this place?

"I've already written it up." Derek headed off his argument. "You can settle with Tanner later."

"All right," he surrendered gracefully, "but I'm buying you a beer next time we're in town."

"Now that I can accept." Walter shook Keith's hand and handed him the two oversized shopping bags.

Chrissy stopped him on his way out, leaning forward to show off as much cleavage as her boat-necked T-shirt allowed. "How about me? You gonna buy me a drink, too?"

It was always easier to deflect than reject. He'd learned that a long time ago. "I would, darlin'," he said, pulling out his best Texas charm, "but I suspect your granddaddy has a shotgun hidden among those boots and coats, and I'm rather attached to my hide, what with all the new clothes and all."

She laughed and straightened up. "Too bad. It would've been worth it."

"I have no doubt, sweetheart."

"Suppose it's for the best. Wouldn't want Tanner getting jealous."

"True. I have to live with the man. Wouldn't want him to think I was coming on to his girl."

"Oh, I'm not his girl."

He was prevented from pursuing it further by the arrival of the man himself. "Hey, Chrissy," he greeted her before turning to Keith. "I'm starved. Did you get everything?"

"And then some."

"You have enough?"

"Uh, yeah, about that…"

"Derek put it on my tab." Tanner grinned. "Always does."

"So why didn't you say so before?"

"I wanted to see how you did with the old man. How'd he do?" he directed the last to Chrissy.

"Taking him out for a beer."

"Not bad."

"I'm still not getting a beer."

"Keep trying, honey. Eventually, someone will bite."

Once outside, Keith said, "They're a nice family."

"The Walters are good people. Chrissy's fun, too. If a bit overeager at times. But, man, can she play pool."

"Is that a warning?"

Tanner grinned at him. "Depends on how well you play pool."

"Where are we going?"

"I told you, I'm starved. It's time for lunch."

"Tanner, we've got a lot to get done yet. You need to open a business bank account and we need to get started on the articles of incorporation—"

"Which is why we're going to the diner. This is a small town, Keith, and it's lunchtime. Joe Rand from the bank is going to be there getting an open-face roast beef sandwich, and my attorney Jon Woznik is biting into a Reuben. Now come on before all the pie is gone."

"I suppose the town doctor is there as well."

"No. It's the second Tuesday of the month—clinic day at the reservation."

"This really is a different world."

"But not a bad one."

"No," he had to agree. "Just different."

The diner was like every other one he'd been to—shiny on the outside and last decorated several decades ago on the inside. But it was clean and the furnishings were in good condition.

It was busy, probably the only busy establishment in town, but the two of them managed to find seats at the counter.

"Hey, Tanner. The usual?" a pot-bellied man with lively dark eyes asked as he reached their end.

"Do I ever order anything else, Ted?"

"No, but I don't like to assume." He turned to Keith. "You must be Tanner's latest. What'll you be having?"

Keith hadn't even had a chance to look at a menu. He wasn't sure there actually *was* a menu. "What's good?"

"Well, Mabel's had a pot roast going since this morning that smells pretty tasty."

"Sounds good. I'll have that."

"You got it."

As soon as Ted was gone, Keith turned to Tanner. "Do you bring all your government witnesses here?"

"Like you said, there isn't really anywhere else to go."

Ted was back a minute later with coffee. Apparently, there wasn't an option they'd drink something else. Ted winked at him and moved on.

It took a few minutes, but Keith started to realize everyone in the place was watching them.

"All right, how long until they stop?" he asked.

"Stop what?"

"Staring at me."

"They aren't staring at you."

"Seeing as they know you, Tanner, I doubt you're the person of interest."

Tanner shrugged and sipped his coffee. "Might be both of us."

"Why would they be staring at both of us?"

"Who knows?" Tanner still didn't look at him. "Small town people are strange."

"A minute ago you loved small town people."

"Doesn't mean they aren't strange."

"I'm beginning to think you're strange."

"That goes without saying."

Their food came faster than Keith would have expected, and they both stopped talking to eat. The beef was incredible, moist and tender, the mashed potatoes still just a little lumpy to say these were made from the real thing.

He was about halfway through when they were interrupted again.

A tall, willowy man with black curls and pale eyes clapped Tanner on the shoulder. "I wondered when you were going to be in town again."

Tanner swallowed and wiped his mouth. "You know me. I can only resist Mabel's pies for so long. Jonathan Woznik, meet Keith Martin. Keith is my new business manager."

Woznik offered him an equally firm handshake, although Keith thought he saw disappointment around the man's mouth. "Pleased to meet you. You're here to get our boy's affairs in order?"

"Trying to. How did you let him go so long without incorporating?"

"You haven't been around him long if you think 'let' factors in when it comes to Tanner."

"We never discussed incorporation," Tanner interrupted defensively.

"As you'll recall, at the closing when you bought the place, I mentioned that for an operation the size you were looking to create, incorporation might be a good idea."

"Well, there's your problem." Keith was enjoying Tanner being the uncomfortable one for a change. "You gave him an option."

"And you aren't, I take it."

"Not on this."

"Excellent! I'll get the paperwork started. You boys come by the end of next week and we can get the polish on it."

"See, that was relatively painless," Keith said when they were alone again. "You'll likely get more back on your taxes, not to mention making them easier to do."

"And if the business goes under, I might walk away with my shirt."

"Exactly. Optimist."

A stocky man dropped onto the stool beside Keith. "Jonathan tells me you've knocked some sense into Tanner here."

"It hasn't come to blows. Yet," Keith replied. "Would you be Joe Rand?"

"Right in one."

He looked at Tanner. "Did someone overhear us in the street?"

"Or maybe I made some phone calls on the way to meet you."

"The town is small, but not that small," Rand interjected. "My assistant is drawing up the papers as we speak. So when you boys are done, stop on by the bank. No rush."

Then he was gone.

You boys. Like they were an item or something. People were strange indeed.

Keith turned to Tanner. "Anyone else stopping by, or am I going to be able to finish my lunch in peace?"

"Just one. And be nice. How are you, Mabel?"

There was no way the old woman standing on the other side of the counter ran the diner's busy kitchen. It just wasn't possible. Her skin was translucent, and her bones underneath the thin covering of muscle looked as if they'd break if you looked at her wrong. But there was an implacable glint in her eye that said they'd take her out of her kitchen on a stretcher. To a hearse.

"So? What did the big city Texas boy think of my food?"

"I'd tell you, ma'am, if I got a chance to eat."

"Yeah, you boys don't get much of a chance to eat first time in. Don't worry; you'll get plenty of chances to get sick of my cooking."

"If the potatoes are always like this, somehow I doubt it."

It was a simple compliment, but it did the trick. "You like pie? Of course you like pie. What man doesn't like pie? No matter how funny. Ted, get Tanner's boyfriend a piece of the cherry before it's all gone, you hear?"

"Hey!" Tanner protested. "I wanted the cherry!"

"I'm not Tanner's boyfriend."

Everyone in the diner stopped. All that was missing was a needle scratching across a record.

Mabel was the one to break the silence. "Damn, it's about time Chrissy had a shot with one of your boys, Tanner. Nicely done."

"Wait, I thought Chrissy and he—" Keith's head was spinning.

"Oh, sugar, you're cute, but clueless."

"Tanner, what's she talking about?"

"Yeah. I meant to tell you—"

But he didn't need to say anything. Keith had finally, finally figured it out. In front of the whole damn town.

He put down his fork and stormed out of the restaurant.

To think he'd actually felt guilty the other night. No wonder everyone in the diner had been staring. How long before the dumb city boy figured it out? *Well, fuck them all.*

"Keith, wait." Tanner jogged across the street to catch up with him.

"Fuck off."

"Well, now you know, that's a possibility."

He whirled on Tanner. "You knew? About me?"

Tanner slipped his hands into his coat pocket. "It came up."

"It came up. It *came up?*" With less of an audience, it was easier to vent his feelings.

"There's not much you can hide from the government."

"Fucking Marta."

"Easy now. That's my cousin you're talking about," Tanner warned.

Keith really didn't care. "You two must've had a good laugh about me. Poor dumb Keith, he'll never figure it out."

"That's not what it was."

"No? Then what was it? Another notch in Tanner Bruenig's bedpost? No wonder poor Chrissy can't get any action. Marta's setting you up with all the queers!"

"Marta takes her job very seriously. She may joke about some things, but the safety of her charges comes first. The Marshals Service isn't a dating service."

"Could've fooled me. Oh, wait…"

"It's not like that. I just didn't want you to feel pressured."

"Bullshit. Give me the keys."

"What?"

"Give me the goddamn keys to the goddamn truck."

"You are not driving my truck."

"Then I'll walk back."

"Christ, you're worse than a teenager."

"I've been humiliated in front of the entire fucking town. Give me the keys or I'm walking."

Tanner thought about it, then pulled out his keys. "You're right. I should have said something sooner. Marta left us in a bad spot, and I let it go longer than I should have. I didn't take small town boredom into consideration. There was no expectation on my part where you're concerned. I just wanted to give you a safe place to hide out for a while, I swear."

"But you've slept with other witnesses."

"Yes."

"Just give me the damn keys."

Tanner did. "For God's sake, use the GPS. If you try to navigate by landmarks, you'll end up in Canada."

Keith snatched away the keys and stalked off.

Canada might not be a bad idea.

CHAPTER 10

Keith made it back to Tanner's property without hitting Canada first. He almost panicked when he saw the locked gate on the drive until he realized the key was on the ring Tanner had given him. He parked at the house, ignoring the welcoming whinny Foster gave him from the paddock, and went in the house.

It took Tanner a couple hours more to get home himself. Keith heard the car in the drive, then Tanner talking to someone before the driver left. Keith stayed in his room with the door shut. It might have been as teenagerly as Tanner accused him of being, but he couldn't face Tanner tonight.

Tanner, however, didn't seem inclined to let him sulk in private. To his credit, he knocked first before sticking his head in. "I see you're still pissed. Be that as it may, you've still got chores."

And the teenage analogy went that much further.

Without comment, Keith got up and pushed past Tanner. Grabbing his coat and slipping on his boots, he went outside. Work would provide a distraction, if nothing else.

Tanner didn't follow him out, which meant he had to do all the work himself. Evening chores were easier because he didn't have to muck out the stalls, but he still had to milk the cows and feed everyone and check the chickens and...

What the fuck had happened to his life?

Right, Dad had screwed him over. Again.

Oh sure, Keith had never wanted for anything. Except the freedom to do what he wanted with his life. And who he wanted. But Daddy paid the bills, so it had been an MBA from Harvard and wining and dining the socialites, while pursuing his own pleasures on the down low.

Now, he didn't even have that. No clubs, no Aspen, no Ryan. Just a hick town that laughed at him and a bunch of fucking farm animals.

He caught sight of Foster watching, dark eyes fathomless and sad. And a stray horse who had a crush on him. This just got better by the minute.

Fuck.

He got the cows into their stanchions by bribing them with their dinner, then cleaned them up and attached the milking machines. When the white fluid started making its way down the clear tubes to the chiller, he pulled out his cell.

It was a new phone with a blocked number to protect him from caller IDs. The only numbers programmed in were Marta's and Tanner's, but he wasn't in the mood to talk to either one of them. Instead, he dialed the number he knew by heart.

It rang three times before Ryan answered. "Hello?"

"Hey, it's me."

"Keith? Fuck me, you're the last person I expected. It's like you disappeared off the face of the planet."

"Might as well have," he grumbled.

"I thought you said you weren't supposed to be in touch with me anymore? That marshal seemed pretty insistent."

"Screw them. After everything they've put me through, I deserve one phone call."

"Where are you?"

He looked around at the cows and the horses and the bales of straw and bags of feed and just started laughing. "You wouldn't believe me if I told you."

"Try me."

"A farm in the middle of nowhere. I'm a fucking farmhand."

Ryan chuckled. "You, doing manual labor? I'd pay to see that."

"I'm sitting in a barn right now in the middle of Montana, milking cows and feeding horses. It's like some god-awful reality show come to life."

"Except then you'd have a chance at fame and a hefty paycheck."

"Yeah, you don't want to know what the government thinks is reasonable for a stipend."

"No more bi-weekly manicures then?"

Keith studied his left hand. Chapped, dirt under the nails, not to mention calluses. "I hate my father."

"Don't we all?"

Keith sighed. "How's life in the real world been?"

"The usual. Good food, good wine, good music. A little less good sex now you're gone."

"A little?"

"Well, you did say to get on with my life."

"Thanks, Ryan. You always were great at making me feel special."

"Life's short. What did you expect?"

"Oh, that maybe you'd miss me?"

"I do miss you, Keith."

"So who is he?"

"No one you'd know."

"I've only been gone three weeks, Ryan. I know everyone. So who is he?"

"Gabriel Conde."

"Wow." He knew Conde was the son of one of the most influential international traders in Houston, rich, handsome and charming. Keith hadn't realized he was gay. *Typical.* "Who was waiting for the opportunity on that one, you or him?"

"Definitely him. After you missed a couple of must-be-seen events, he bought me a drink. You had said move on, so I figured I might as well move up at the same time."

"Always keeping your eye on the prize."

"Not all of us were born into money."

The cows were almost done, but Keith didn't want to get off the phone. "I miss you."

"Please. The first hot body to cross your path will make you forget all about me."

Said hot body was currently cooking dinner. All Tanner had done was humiliate him and make him feel guilty. For what, though, he wondered. Ryan had moved on, and without a backward glance from the sounds of it.

"Still."

"I know. I'd come up to visit, but I think Billings is a little far north for me."

"And I'm six hours farther north than that."

"Six hours? Holy shit, why didn't they just move you to Canada?"

"They practically did." One of the cows mooed uncomfortably. "Look, I've got to go. But it was good talking to you."

"Call again. Keith. Any time. I mean it."

"I will. 'Bye."

The phone call was not supposed to make him feel worse. Calling Ryan had been stupid for a lot of reasons. Then again, maybe it was good to know they were done. Really done.

But he still had to deal with Tanner.

That wasn't a loaded statement at all.

CHAPTER 11

Tanner had just set the food on the table when Keith came in.

"I'm sorry," Keith said.

Not exactly what Tanner had been expecting.

"You were wrong, but I had no right to blow up like I did. Made an even bigger fool of myself."

"Mabel made me bring a whole pie home; she felt so bad for you."

Keith stared at him, astonished.

"No one was laughing at you, Keith. I think they were just all glad I wasn't out here on my own anymore and wanted to get to know you."

"I guess I'm surprised they're so okay with you being gay."

Tanner smirked. "Oh, there are a few assholes around. But when your circle is so small, it's better to be open-minded than not." Then he added, "Also helps that the mayor's son came out a few years before I moved in. A local paving the road goes a long way toward making things easier for the rest of us."

"Did you sleep with him?"

The question wasn't entirely unwarranted, but it hurt nonetheless. "No. Bobby was already involved with someone from college."

"But if he hadn't been, you would have."

In other words, Keith thought he'd sleep with anyone with a dick who seemed amenable. "Bobby's a bit too idealistic for my tastes."

"Meaning young?"

"Very young. Painfully young. Are you going to eat? The food's getting cold, and I'm starving."

"Do you always think with your stomach?"

"It's better than other things."

That earned him a small smile. "You have a point."

They both sat and ate in relative silence.

Tanner took the risk of initiating conversation. "So you didn't have any trouble getting home?"

"I was good and did everything the voice on the dashboard told me. At least the gate key was on your key ring or I'd have been screwed."

"There's a spare on the back of the post if you ever need it."

"Now you tell me."

"Hey, you were pissed. I wasn't sure you were going to hear anything I said."

"I would have heard, but ignored it out of spite." After taking a bite, Keith asked, "Who brought you home?"

"Chrissy."

Keith almost choked on his food. "Going for the irony?"

"Going for the person who could get away in the middle of the afternoon. Oh, and here..." Tanner handed Keith the thick envelope he'd left on the counter.

"What's this?"

"The new bank account. Since I was stuck in town, I figured I might as well get it done."

"Shit, I forgot about that. And the computer."

"Boxes are in the den. Waiting for you. It's your pet project; you can do the work."

Keith looked as if Christmas had come early.

Since they seemed to be on better footing, Tanner took the chance. "I am sorry for what happened. I certainly never meant it to come out the way it did."

"What did you think would happen?"

"I don't know. You'd get comfortable here, let something slip and then I could say, 'Really? Me, too!' and then we'd go from there."

"Life's never that accommodating."

"You'd think I would have figured it out by now."

Keith set down his fork. "Look, about what I said in town—"

"I haven't slept with all my charges," Tanner cut him off. "People make assumptions when there's a guy here, just like they did with you. But I did sleep with some of them. It was purely consensual and never *quid pro quo*. I don't have any expectations of you, Keith, honestly. I just want to keep you safe."

"And if I did want something to happen?"

His tone was unreadable, not giving Tanner any ideas how to play this. Which left honesty, he supposed. "Then it'd be up to you to make the first move."

"That doesn't tell me whether or not you're interested."

"Telling would take all the fun out of it."

"In other words, we're both stubborn bastards and neither of us is going to get any." Amusement crinkled the corners of Keith's eyes.

"Sounds about right."

Keith wiped his mouth and pushed away from the counter. "Then I guess I'd better get to work on that computer."

Tanner let him go.

He took his time finishing dinner, then cleaning up. After...well, there wasn't anything else to distract himself with.

Poking his head into the den, he found Keith absorbed in setting up the computer, lost in a tangle of wires and plastic. Tanner decided not to interrupt him.

Instead, he grabbed a couple beers and headed for the living room. There had to be a decent game going on somewhere. No telling what tomorrow would bring, so he might as well relax and guarantee himself a decent night's sleep.

The Jazz were playing the Timberwolves at home, so Tanner settled in for what promised to be a mediocre game. From the other room, he could hear boxes tearing, the clatter of components, and Keith cursing often. It probably would have been more entertaining to go watch him, but Tanner figured it would be better to leave him alone tonight.

Keith emerged during the third quarter and Tanner's second beer. "It's up and running, and you won't know how you lived without it." He perched on the far arm of the couch. "How's the game?"

"I've seen worse."

"That exciting?"

"Pretty much." Tanner took a sip and motioned toward the kitchen. "There's more in the fridge. Help yourself."

"Thanks. I think I will."

Instead of getting up to go to the kitchen, he leaned over to lick the last drops off Tanner's lips before kissing him properly.

About fucking time.

Too soon, Keith pulled back, eyes dark. "Is that a clear enough first move?"

"You don't hear me complaining." He caught Keith by the back of the head and pulled him down for more.

Keith relaxed into it instantly, his body pressing against Tanner's, his mouth soft and mobile. The sounds of the game faded, and all Tanner could hear was the sound of Keith's breath and the soft pulls of their mouths coming together and separating again and again and again.

When Keith straddled him, Tanner groaned.

Keith chuckled. "Easy now, I'm barely getting started."

"God, you're one of those, aren't you?"

"One of what?"

Tanner tugged Keith's shirts free from his jeans. "One of those who takes it slow and likes to drive his partner crazy."

"All depends on the day." He pressed a tender kiss below Tanner's Adam's apple. "Don't you think you deserve it?"

"I prefer to do the driving."

"Prefer...but you're open to mixing things up?"

"Like you said. I deserve it."

"Are you taking responsibility for this?"

"For my part. Marta's partially to blame, too, remember?"

"I'm not going to fuck Marta."

"She'll be crushed."

"I'm sure she'll get over it." Keith's mouth was more demanding this time when he kissed Tanner.

Tanner welcomed it, following every step Keith led. He worked his way under the hem of Keith's shirt to caress the taut, shifting muscles of his back, while Keith controlled his head as he explored every aspect of Tanner's mouth.

"I'm not complaining," Tanner said when he had the chance, "but why the change of heart? The way things were earlier, I thought you were going to stay holed up in your room for the rest of your stay."

"Did some thinking. And I didn't like being a teenager when I was one, so..."

Tanner captured his mouth in another exploratory kiss. He suspected there was more to it than that, but what did it really matter?

They took their time. There was nothing desperate about it, although it certainly was hungry. When Keith finished with the buttons on Tanner's shirt and stroked his hands over Tanner's bare chest for the first time, they both moaned, their kisses becoming more eager. When he started on Tanner's belt, Tanner caught his wrist to stop him. "Are we doing this here?"

Keith kissed Tanner's shoulder. "I don't see why not."

"Condoms are in the bedroom."

"We'll get there. I have other things in mind first."

"Oh?"

"Mmm." He rose up on his knees and undid his own jeans, drawing out his cock that, unlike the other night, now stood at full erection, thick and straight and tempting. "You want to make up to me for today, don't you?"

Tanner watched Keith's face as he took hold of Keith's cock. To his satisfaction, Keith's eyes drifted closed, a satisfied smile curling his mouth. "Like this?" He started stroking it lazily.

"It's a nice start."

Tanner kept a steady pace. "You think you're calling the shots here?"

"Right now?" Keith peeked one eye open. "Definitely."

Tanner released him long enough to whip Keith's T-shirt off before returning to his attention, now with the very attractive landscape of Keith's chest to enjoy. He only had to lean forward a few bare inches to taste the shape of each muscle and curve.

There was the faintest hint of salt over the subtle spiciness of Keith's skin. "So good," he murmured as he eased Keith back, working his way down to the dick he'd fantasized about.

It wasn't going to work from this angle, though, so Tanner lifted Keith to set his bare ass on the coffee table, shoving his jeans farther down. Keith leaned back, supporting himself on his hands, gripping the far edge of the table, and watched as Tanner slid to his knees in front of him.

On second thought, the jeans needed to go altogether. Tugging them off, he earned a low, throaty chuckle from Keith.

"You're nothing if not thorough."

"I like room to maneuver."

Keith spread his legs in invitation, offering him plenty of room.

Taking his time, Tanner ran his hands up Keith's calves to his thighs. Coarse hair added just the right contrast to toned muscle and warm skin.

"I'm still mad at you." Keith already sounded breathless.

"Okay." Tanner kissed him high on the inside of his thigh.

"I don't care how good a blow you give me."

"I might change your mind." He copied the gesture on the other side before trailing his tongue up through the thicket of dark hair to tease at Keith's balls.

Keith tensed slightly, but sighed. "You can try."

"I aim to do more than try."

He took his time, tracking how all the pieces of Keith's body came together, completely masculine and oh so sensitive. Keith was more responsive than Tanner had fantasized, squirming and rising under Tanner's attentions, vocal but far from verbal. His repertoire of grunts and gasps, soft moans and wordless groans was enough to make Tanner ache for more.

At last, he turned his attention fully to Keith's cock, keeping to the same thorough exploration.

Keith raked his fingers through Tanner's hair to hold him in place, his other hand still supporting him as he rocked under Tanner's ministrations. Tanner let Keith set the pace, speeding up as his hips accelerated, until the sounds of wet suction and skin slapping against wood filled the room.

Porn got it wrong. This was the way Tanner liked it, noisy and wet and messy and reeking, not silent and clinical like the movies. And Keith was anything but silent.

"Fuck, Tanner, I can't—"

"Don't," Tanner said before redoubling his efforts.

He'd barely worked a second finger past the tight iris of Keith's ass before the man came, muscles clenching around Tanner's digits and promising all sorts of wonderful things for when his dick was there.

"God damn it."

Tanner hadn't expected Keith to sound upset. "What? Did I—"

Keith shut him up with a kiss, sliding off the table to join him on the floor. "I was planning to fuck you first," he complained half-heartedly.

"Oh, is that all?" Tanner grinned. "I can promise you plenty of opportunities to make up for it."

"But I still won't be first." He slipped a hand between them to caress Tanner's hard-on. "Unless you're planning to let this go to waste."

"Would you?"

"Fuck, no."

Tanner dragged Keith into a deep, soul-searching kiss as he rocked into Keith's firm grip. "There's your answer."

"We'd better get to the bedroom then, don't you think?"

Tanner hated to move. He was comfortable where they were and didn't want to break the intimacy they'd built. But the way Keith was stroking him, he wasn't going to last long if they didn't.

Which was probably his intention.

Reluctantly, he nudged Keith up and climbed to his feet.

Rather than let him go, Tanner kicked off his pants and pulled Keith into another kiss, indulging in the feel of their naked bodies in full contact. "I'm sorry I didn't tell you sooner," he said, words soft against Keith's mouth.

"We could've been doing this all along."

And things would have been a hell of a lot easier. None of which mattered now.

Gradually, he maneuvered them to his room.

Backing Keith up, Tanner tripped him into the half-made bed and followed him down, looking forward to feeling Keith writhing beneath him as Tanner fucked him. "If you really want to go first, we can stop."

Keith gave him a shove. "Get the fucking rubbers."

Tanner wasn't about to argue. A few moments later, he had the condom on and slicked up.

"How do you want me?"

Grinning, Tanner urged Keith's knees up and spread him wide. "Exactly like this."

"I was hoping you'd say that."

Tanner took up Keith's blatant invitation, their cocks dueling as Tanner fingered Keith's ass again, getting him ready.

"Christ, that feels good."

"You sound surprised." The tight muscles resisted a third finger for the briefest moment before allowing it in, making Keith groan.

"Haven't gotten fucked for quite a while."

It hadn't even crossed Tanner's mind that Keith might not—

"I like it, don't worry. Ryan was just…a really horrible top."

"Ryan, huh? Should I be jealous?"

Keith took hold of Tanner's cock and guided him in. "Oh definitely. Especially if it makes you screw me harder."

"You like it rough, do you?"

Keith nipped at Tanner's lip. "Do your worst."

Tanner was more than happy to oblige, sinking into Keith's tight ass without hesitation.

"Just like that." Keith groaned. "Had enough slow and easy for one night."

"If I'd known you wanted it rough, I'd have put you on your knees." It was easy to give Keith what he wanted. Tanner had wanted it himself for so long it was hard to hold back.

"No, you wouldn't. You'd still have done it like this. The first time."

That Keith could read him so well in such a short time should have been disconcerting. Rather than think on it too much, Tanner caught Keith's mouth again and effectively shut them both up as he lost himself in the pleasures of the flesh.

Keith clung to him, encouraging every stroke, fingers digging into his shoulder blades for purchase, legs levering against the back of his thighs to demand each pounding thrust. Tanner couldn't think. He was only aware of Keith beneath him, wanting him and giving him everything they both wanted so fucking badly.

Tanner's life didn't allow for regrets. But if it did, damn if he wouldn't regret not saying something sooner.

Aroused as he was, with such a punishing pace, holding out for a short while wasn't even in the realm of possibility. He'd barely glimpsed the wonders Keith's body held before he came hard, slamming into Keith one last time.

Keith chuckled, holding him close as he shuddered to completion. "Been holding onto that one for a while, haven't you?"

"Jerking off isn't the same." Groaning, he pulled out and flopped down next to Keith. "Christ, that felt good."

"You aren't kidding."

"We really should've done this sooner."

"Again, you'll get no argument from me."

"Any regrets?"

"Only if you keep talking."

Tanner shut up, but only for a moment. "You hungry?"

"Mabel's pie?"

"Yeah."

"Sounds good." Keith pushed himself up off the bed. "Bring the condoms."

Tanner grinned. The winter was looking up.

CHAPTER 12

Keith woke up to Tanner kissing his way down his chest and fondling his balls.

As these things went, it was a good way to wake up.

Tanner must have realized he was awake as well. "God, you're a heavy sleeper."

Keith didn't open his eyes. "Maybe you weren't trying hard enough."

Shifting, Tanner covered Keith's body with his. "If I tried any harder, you'd have woken up with a cock up your ass."

Finally, Keith cracked one eye open. "You say that like it's a bad thing."

"It spoils the fun if you aren't awake to enjoy it."

Keith skimmed a hand down Tanner's back. "Oh, I'm sure I'd wake up at some point."

"I'll keep that in mind for next time." He lowered his head to tease at Keith's mouth. Judging by the erection digging into Keith's leg, next time was coming fast.

Last night had been decadent. They had fucked and eaten and showered and screwed and eaten some more before ending up back in bed for one last, slow fuck that had left Keith more relaxed than he'd been in months. Waking up next to Tanner was proving to be the icing on the cake. Or the promise of another sinful day.

Holding Tanner close, Keith levered himself off the bed and rolled Tanner onto his back. "My turn."

Tanner grinned and stretched his arms up in surrender. "Be my guest."

Keith wasn't interested in being patient or gentle, rubbing his hand roughly over Tanner's cock and balls as he kissed him, his tongue thrusting into Tanner's mouth in promise of what was to come.

And then the alarm went off.

Tanner cursed and reached for it. "We have to go milk the cows."

"Later." Keith tried to capture his mouth again, but Tanner dodged him.

"We can't later. It has to be now or they'll get off their schedule and we'll lose production." Tanner shoved him off and sat up.

Keith really hated farm life, but Tanner was right. Intellectually, Keith understood and agreed. The rest of him, however, wasn't remotely pleased.

He grumbled the whole time he was getting dressed and continued to do so on the way out to the barn, where he took on the mucking, while Tanner saw to the cows. It was dirty and physical and fit his mood at the moment.

At least the weather had improved. The sun shone brightly, unhindered by any clouds or trees for miles, and the temperature was in the mid-fifties, comfortable enough for him to work in shirtsleeves. Keith rolled the last wheelbarrow load of used straw out to the compost and paused to admire the view.

"See, there are some upsides to this life," Tanner said as he joined him.

The mountains in the distance were nothing like the gray Keith had always envisioned. In the sunlight, even at this distance they were mottled blue and rust, white peaks gradating down to the sere plains. "That song never made any sense to me before, but there it is. Purple mountains and fruited plains."

Tanner slipped his arms around him. "You should see it in the spring," he said softly near Keith's ear. "The grasses are all greening up and the wildflowers start blooming and flocks of cranes are stopping off on their migration north. It's just about the most beautiful thing I've ever seen."

Keith twisted his neck around to look at Tanner. "You really love it here, don't you?"

Tanner never took his eyes off the horizon. "Yeah, I really do."

Keith turned back, trying to see the landscape through Tanner's eyes.

When Tanner kissed his neck, it startled him. He soon relaxed, enjoying Tanner's presence. "Just when I think I have you figured out, you surprise me."

"I'm not that hard to figure out." He didn't stop, mouth trailing over the nape of Keith's neck to nuzzle at the other side.

"I know. I keep thinking you're running some bigger game like everyone in Houston does, but you're not. You're...simple."

Tanner lifted his head. "I'm not sure, but I think I might be insulted."

Keith smirked. "Bad word choice. What I mean is you don't have an ulterior motive."

"I wouldn't say that." Tanner rocked his hips forward, arousal unmistakable.

"Apart from the obvious."

"Life's too short for games." He began nipping along Keith's jaw more insistently, hands coming up to caress his chest. "I work hard, I play hard, and when I want something, I ask for it. Usually nicely."

"Usually."

"Keith"—Tanner breathed into his ear—"come back into the barn with me so I can fuck you in the hay."

Cliché as it was, Keith's knees went a bit weak at Tanner's words. "Jesus..."

"I'll take that as a yes." And Tanner led him back to the barn.

Keith was grateful the horses were out. Cows were one thing, but having Foster for an audience would be too much.

Backing Keith up against one of the support beams, Tanner leaned into him and returned to assaulting his neck, this time letting his hands find their way under Keith's shirt. "This might be the last warm day we have," he said, teasing at Keith's Adam's apple, "and I really didn't want to miss out on the opportunity for this."

"I suppose it makes up for having to get out of bed," Keith said as he tugged Tanner's shirt free from his jeans.

"Must be sad to live in a place like Houston where the only place you can have sex is in a boring old bed."

"Yeah, but we make up for it by being really kinky."

"Oh, really?" Tanner had Keith's pants open and was working his way into his briefs.

"I've done things that would blow your mind."

"You think so, huh?" Tanner's work-roughened fingers curled around Keith's cock.

69

He was suddenly slapped by the memory of Ryan, bound and gagged over the arm of his sofa, his ass rosy red from the beating Keith had given him. He channeled the lust the image inspired into devouring Tanner's mouth as he jerked his pants open as well. "But it's probably not your thing."

"All depends." He groaned as Keith caught his dick. "I might surprise you even more."

He caught Tanner's ass with his free hand, hauling him close enough to grind their cocks together. "You want me to get a bridle and saddle out of the tack room, then?"

"It'd sure suit your eyes."

"Not for me."

Tanner grinned. "Could be interesting."

Right then, Keith wanted nothing more than to wrap a pair of leather reins around his fist while he fucked Tanner hard.

Tanner's grip tightened, making Keith groan. "Later."

"That a promise?"

"Yes."

"You're only saying that to get what you want."

"I'm getting what I want anyway." He shoved Keith's hand away to take both their cocks in one broad hand, making Keith twitch hard enough to bang his head against the wooden beam. "I'm going to fuck you right now until you scream loud enough to scare the animals then we can go inside and find out just how deep this kink of yours goes."

Keith clutched at his shoulders. "Christ, fuck me."

Tanner was already shoving him into one of the clean stalls and down onto the loose straw covering the floor. Keith kicked his jeans free and wrapped his legs around Tanner's hips, desperate for penetration.

Tanner seemed equally desperate, quickly rolling a condom down his length and moving into position.

"Don't you dare go slow."

"I have no intention of it." And then he was pressing inside.

Keith groaned, not bothering to hold it back. There was nothing around to hear them but the cows and a few chickens.

"You like that, don't you, Keith?" Tanner was gritting his teeth, already building to a hammering pace. "You like getting to make some noise when you fuck, don't you? No neighbors around here to get offended at how damn loud you are."

Busybody neighbors had a certain appeal, but no one around was even better. Hell, it was liberating.

Tanner's pace became too punishing for words, so they drove each other on through fierce kissing and incoherent sounds.

Keith clutched at the straw, desperate for anything to improve his leverage as his orgasm raced toward him. All there was was Tanner, and Keith clung to him, wailing out ecstatic curses as he came as hard as he had the first time.

Tanner climaxed with a shout and collapsed heavily atop Keith.

They lay there, breathing ragged as they came down.

Keith could really get used to this. And the thought didn't terrify him as much as he expected.

Finally, Tanner rolled off Keith, collapsing bonelessly beside him. "Worth getting out of bed?"

"Fuck, yes."

"I could kill Marta."

"Why?"

"If she hadn't been so busy being secretive, we could've been doing this all along."

Keith looked over at him. "How easy do you think I am?"

Tanner glanced back, still breathing heavily, and laughed.

Keith couldn't help laughing as well.

"Christ, this straw is itchy."

"It was your idea." Keith hadn't actually noticed it until now. He got up, pulling Tanner to his feet. "Come on. I need a shower."

Tanner caught him in a loose embrace. "What about all that stuff you wanted to do?"

"Oh, I still want to do it. But as you keep pointing out, it's going to be a long winter."

"Fair enough."

They dressed quickly, but Tanner finished first, disappearing while Keith was focused on his buttons. He reappeared a moment later, a bridle hanging from one finger. "In case you get an urge later. Or I do."

Later, right. Keith grinned. Life in the middle of nowhere suddenly didn't seem so horrible now.

CHAPTER 13

They settled into a comfortable routine. Every morning, they'd fool around until the alarm went off, then go out to take care of the animals. Usually, they waited until they got back to the house and in the shower before having sex, but sometimes they didn't make it out of the barn. Either way was good. Then breakfast and computer work until one of them got bored and distracted the other. The afternoon went much the same way. Then they'd have dinner; watch a movie or game for a while. The serious stuff they saved for evening, back in Tanner's bed. Keith was good at pushing Tanner's boundaries, but Tanner was finding Keith had some edges of his own worth stretching.

All in all, it was a pretty good life.

They were relaxing in the Jacuzzi one evening in mid-November. The air was cold and crisp, making the stars shine all the brighter in the clear sky.

"I think I could get used to this life," Keith murmured as he watched the near-imperceptible turn of the heavens above them.

"What, the bright lights of the city aren't calling you?"

Keith gestured up at the sky. "Those are some pretty nice lights up there. And there's always Jensen's Crossing when I need some city action."

Tanner snorted. "Jensen's Crossing's got two bars and a liquor store. We don't even have a fast food restaurant. I'd hardly call it a city."

"You've got the important things. Everything else is distraction."

Tanner gave him a sidelong glance. "Have I been working you too hard?"

"Why?"

"That's not something I expected to hear from you."

Keith shrugged, then grabbed his beer.

Tanner sighed. "Well, trust me, come spring, you'll be glad you're nowhere near here. You think this is hard work, but it's got nothing on calving season." He ignored the pang at the thought of Keith leaving.

"There's something to be said about always learning something new every day. My fresh start when this is all over is looking a lot different than it did in the beginning."

"Meaning?"

"I really don't know." Keith grinned. "I just know I won't be seeking out the life I had, and it's kind of…liberating."

"I know that feeling. It's why I ended up out here in the first place. No one telling me what to do, where to go, who to kill. No good guys or bad guys. Just me and several hundred cows. That's freedom."

"The T1 connection, satellite TV, and Jacuzzi don't hurt matters any."

"Well, no."

"And Mabel's pies."

"Yeah."

"And Cecily's cheese."

"Oh, yes. Funny, though, the best reason has only turned up recently."

"Oh?"

Tanner caught Keith by the arm and pulled him onto his lap, the water of the pool making him buoyant and easy to manipulate. "Yeah."

Keith grinned down at him. "No complaints here."

Tanner turned them so Keith's back was against the edge of the tub and settled himself between his legs before catching Keith's mouth in a lingering kiss, tasting the beer they were drinking and the burgers they'd had for dinner and a subtler, indefinable flavor that could only be described as Keith.

Keith held him close, responding with a languid eagerness. The water made their movements near frictionless, keeping in line with the slow build.

Before Keith could stop him, Tanner caught him by the waist and heaved him up out of the water to perch on the edge of the tub.

"Damn it, Tanner, it's cold out here!"

"Yeah, but I can't blow you if your cock is two feet underwater."

"You could always hold your br—" Keith's protest died away as Tanner swallowed him down. "Fuck me."

Later.

Tanner took his time, not too much since it really was cold out and the steam from the tub only offset that somewhat, but enough to savor the experience and render Keith pliant.

He loved doing this. Keith's cock felt so good in his mouth, hard and satiny, ridged with veins and helmet, so many interesting avenues for his tongue to take. And Keith loved it just as much, despite the cold and the snow around them. He braced himself on one arm, the other hand scrubbing through Tanner's hair encouraging, demanding as he watched Tanner go down over and over again.

When Keith began to shiver more noticeably, Tanner redoubled his efforts, soon bringing Keith to a shuddering climax.

Tanner tugged him back into the water, holding him as he recovered. "Love doing that to you."

"What, freezing my ass off?"

"Admit it. You got off on the cold and the hot."

Keith grinned. "No, because you'll keep doing it."

"Trust me. I'm going to keep doing it anyway."

Keith settled the back of his shoulder against Tanner's chest, relaxing in his embrace. "You know, I never expected witness protection to be like this."

"Good?" He ignored the ripple of anxiety he felt.

He needn't have worried. "Are you kidding? Alone in the outback with a sexy, serious, seriously sexy cowboy? Hell, my sex life's never had it so good."

Relaxing, Tanner chuckled. "Who am I to complain about that?"

"That's another thing I like about you. Your modesty."

"Modesty's overrated."

Keith chuckled, the movement sending ripples across the water and vibrating against Tanner's skin. "Oh, so that's why you've stopped dressing around the house."

"Not much point in getting dressed when you're going to be ripping my clothes off me at the first opportunity."

"I—" Keith turned, indignant, but Tanner yanked him into another kiss with a low laugh that quickly turned into a moan when Keith settled on his lap.

Now everything was perfect.

CHAPTER 14

Thanksgiving came quicker than Keith would have believed. The ranch was already covered in a foot of snow with more on the way. But it didn't matter. The house was cozy, the animals all content to be stuck in the paddock and barn and the herds out on the prairie were set up with enough browse to keep them content as winter closed in around them.

He had finally finished all the data input, and he was able to come into his own as Tanner's business manager. Some nights, instead of settling in front of the TV, they'd sit down at the kitchen table and start running numbers for all the different scenarios Tanner had in his head. Making recommendations on land leases, diversified crops, herd expansion and the rest made Keith feel more like a part of things than just a farmhand, easily replaced. The fact Tanner actually listened and took his advice was an amazing boost to his ego as well.

Two days before Thanksgiving, Marta called. "Hey, guy, I wanted to check in with you before the holidays got crazy."

"It's not so crazy from where I'm sitting."

"That's because you and Tanner have a pass from the big family Thanksgiving. Those of us who aren't currently in hiding are expected to appear at Gran's house in Denver no matter what end of the earth we're currently at."

"Gee, I'm sorry to miss it."

"You are such a liar. Everything okay there?"

"Everything's great."

"Yeah, I've been hearing some of how great it is."

He refused to blush. "Tanner's got a big mouth."

"He's never been able to keep any secrets from me. If it makes you feel any better, this time seems to be greater than any of the others."

Keith smiled. "Good to have an unbiased opinion on that, then."

"Are you?" She hesitated. "Keith, any idea why your old boyfriend would be trying to get in touch with you?"

He'd known deep down that one call would bite him in the ass eventually. "Uh, Ryan's trying to get in touch?"

Separated by however many hundreds of miles, Keith could tell Marta saw right through him. "What aren't you telling me, Keith?"

"Nothing, honestly," he lied. "Is he okay?"

"Well, he didn't ask for protection, so presumably he hasn't been targeted. But he knows he can't be in touch with you. I'm not happy he's trying."

"No, me neither." It actually wasn't a lie. Keith had moved on now, pretty significantly since their last conversation. "He'll give up if you stonewall him long enough."

"I still don't like it."

"If I know Ryan, he probably broke up with his latest trust-fund baby and he's falling back on old habits, trying to call me to whine about it. Always has."

"He used to do that a lot?"

"Constantly. Ryan lives for drama."

"All right, well, I'll look into it. You boys have a good Thanksgiving. I'm still hoping to get up there for Christmas, but we'll see what happens. In the meantime, I'll check back in next week."

"Sounds good, Marta. Happy Thanksgiving."

"You, too, Keith."

Shit, damn, fuck. Keith was dialing the number before he could think twice. It would be quick and they'd both move on.

"This is Ryan."

"What in the hell are you doing trying to get in touch with me?"

He sounded petulant. "I missed you. I wanted to talk."

"Damn it, Ryan, I'm in hiding! What part of that don't you understand?"

"It didn't keep you from calling me when you were lonely."

He had a point. "All right, you're right. I'm sorry. But for God's sake, going through my marshal? Who's pissed as hell, by the way. You might want to tell her the Escaveras *are* after you. It would be safer than dealing with her when she's angry."

"Well, how else am I supposed to reach you? It's not like you gave me a number or even an email address."

"Because I wasn't supposed to. There's no point in us both being in danger." Especially since they'd both moved on.

"We were friends before we were lovers, Keith."

Friend of convenience was more apt. And why had it taken him this long to realize just how much Ryan had used him over the years. "I'm sorry, Ryan. This has to be goodbye."

"So it's okay for you to leave your little fortress of solitude when it suits you, but God forbid I ask for a little attention." Ryan was sounding angrier and a little desperate.

"What do you want from me, Ryan? I'm hell and gone out in god-forsaken Montana! It's not like I can come over for a comfort fuck."

"You always were a selfish bastard, Keith. Enjoy fucking the sheep there in BFE." The line went dead.

Keith sat there with the phone in his hand. "Good riddance," he said, chucking the phone on his bed and getting up. Tanner would be back from town soon and there were chores to do.

He regretted things had to end like this. He and Ryan had been close once, or what Keith would have considered close another lifetime ago. But that life was gone, and more and more, Keith was finding he didn't wish to have it back.

Foster whickered to him from the paddock, eager for his evening treat and scratch behind the ear. And he thought off in the distance he heard the sound of Tanner's truck rattling up the frozen drive.

This was his life now, and he was a better man for it.

For the first time that he could remember, Keith almost wanted to thank his father for running afoul of the Escaveras. Sure, there had to be easier ways for making a fresh start, but the whole situation was beginning to feel like a blessing more than a curse.

Tanner joined him in the barn just as he was finishing up with the milking. "Hey." He dropped the heavy bag of feed he carried onto the diminished stack by the door.

"Hey there." Keith finished stripping water out of the sterilized hoses. "How was town?"

"About the same."

"And what kind of pie did Mabel send me?"

Tanner grinned. "Cherry. Your favorite. I don't know what you did to charm her so much. She never used to send me home with pie."

"Why should she? You go in and buy every time you're in town. But me, I'm stuck here, alone on this big, empty farm with no companionship but you. Who wouldn't feel bad for me?"

"Me, you big baby."

"Thanks a lot."

As they walked to the house, Tanner asked, "So, did I miss anything exciting?"

"Marta called for her weekly check-in and to complain how you get out of family Thanksgiving." *Among other things.*

He chuckled. "She's never forgiven me for the years I missed by being in Afghanistan. Like I did it on purpose or something."

"A man who chooses to live out in the middle of nowhere, well away from family, yeah, she's crazy to think that."

Tanner elbowed him. "Watch it or I'll feed the pie to the horses."

"And break Mabel's heart?"

"Yeah, but maybe Foster will pay me some attention for a change."

"Jealous?"

"Yes." Tanner pulled Keith into a loose embrace and kissed him, light and tender, but with a casual intimacy entirely new to Keith.

This was his life now. Cherry pie, a stalker horse and this man.

And damn him if he wasn't enjoying it.

CHAPTER 15

"You sure you won't come into town with me?" Tanner closed up the back of the truck and came around to where Keith was leaning on the door.

"I need to get those bids out today if we're going to have the new equipment by spring. It's getting late as it is. Besides, between Thanksgiving dinner and Mabel's pies, I'm loading on the pounds. Better to stay away from temptation."

"Loading on the pounds, my ass." Tanner caught Keith around the waist and pulled him closer. "You look better than you did when you got here, and to be honest, you looked pretty damn good then."

He loved the way Keith relaxed into him, draping his arms around Tanner's shoulders. "Flattery will get you nowhere."

"Which is why I don't bother." He kissed Keith quickly, but then tore himself away. "I should be back by two or three. Then, if you're really worried about your weight, we can burn off some of those calories the fun way."

Keith grinned. "Can't wait."

"And I'll tell Mabel not to bother with the pie."

"Then don't bother coming back."

Tanner chuckled and started up the truck.

Things were getting comfortable, natural for them, and Tanner had to admit, he liked it. He had noticed the way Keith had said "we" when talking about the new farm equipment they had decided to invest in. As if it was important to him and he was going to be here to see it happen.

More and more, Tanner was finding he wanted it that way. To his surprise, it wasn't scary at all.

The Christmas lights were up all over town, the tree in the square bedecked and beribboned for the holidays. In this era of Internet shopping, there wasn't a whole lot of hustle and bustle in town, but there was still a sense of anticipation. More smiling faces, less grim determination.

He finished the banking quickly and met Joseph Red Deer to send paychecks out to the reservation to the guys who tended Tanner's herd before heading over to the feed store. They needed more chicken feed, in addition to the grain for the horses and cows. He got caught up on the news from Karl Lovig, who owned the store, and Tim Kleven, whose family had the ranch a couple miles down the road and across from Tanner's. It took him longer than he'd intended, but he knew better than to miss stopping by the diner. Mabel would have his balls faster than Keith would. Besides, he was starving.

He could tell something was off when he stepped inside the dinner. The background hum of conversation was all but absent and a faint tension ran through the air. He found the cause seated in the back corner booth. Strangers tended to be fairly welcome in Jensen's Crossing, as long as they were courteous. These three men, however, wouldn't be openly welcomed anywhere. They gave off a clear "don't fuck with us" vibe, every bit as difficult to ignore as their "casual" designer clothes. It was difficult to blend in when you wore the best money could buy. Then again, these people didn't want to blend in.

Tanner took a seat at the counter, keeping half an eye on the strangers.

Ted brought him coffee without a word.

Wrapping his hand around the cup, Tanner turned his head away from the corner booth. "How long have they been here?" he asked under his breath.

Ted started wiping the counter. "About an hour. There are two more around town. Derek called to tell me they'd been in the store, see if I knew who they were."

"They say anything?"

"Not these three. The other two are looking for Keith Lewis. Say their old friends of his and heard he was in the area."

"How long ago did Derek call?"

"About twenty minutes."

Meaning they might no longer be in town and already on their way out to the ranch. But rushing off would do as much harm as good, as he was more than certain the three in the corner had their eye on him. He needed to get a message to Keith without arousing their suspicion.

"I gotta take a leak," he announced to the whole room, standing up. "Bring me a burger and some fries, will you?"

Ted nodded, carefully not looking at the strangers as he turned to put the order in.

Mabel was watching Tanner as he passed the kitchen door, accusing, pleading. He was tempted to go in and comfort her, but these guys weren't going to do anything here. Keith was the one in danger.

It was a two-stall bathroom, so there wasn't a lock on the door. He went into one of the stalls and shut the door, pulling out his phone to dial Keith's number. After five rings, there was no answer. Frustrated, he punched the disconnect button and dialed the house number. Still no answer.

"Keith," he ordered the answering machine when it picked up, "there are guys here in town looking for you. I want you to take the Land Rover and get out to the reservation right now. The cops there can look out for you until I can get there. I'll be at the house in forty-five minutes. Go now." He disconnected again and called Marta. He didn't even wait for her to speak. "There are guys here," he snapped. "Escavera guys. They know Keith's real name and they're looking for him."

"Shit. It'll be three hours before I can get anyone there."

"Well, get them here. I don't want them threatening anyone in town. I'm taking him out to—"

The door to the restroom opened, and he saw a pair of highly polished dress shoes come in the bathroom from under the door.

He disconnected and turned off the ringer before flushing the toilet and coming out.

The man didn't bother to hide what he was doing, just stood in the corner and watched Tanner wash his hands as nonchalantly as he could. Tanner nodded to him briefly before going back out to the counter.

He wasn't alone for long.

"I don't suppose you'd know where Keith Lewis might be staying." The man's tone was pleasant enough.

"Keith, did you say? Lewis?" Tanner frowned as if in thought. "No, can't say as I've run into a Keith around these parts."

"You're Tanner Bruenig?"

"Yeah."

"Funny, Mr. Bruenig, but the girl down at the hardware store said your new business manager is named Keith. Keith Martin."

Damn it, Chrissy.

"Martin and Lewis. That's funny. Someone was being clever. He come into town with you?"

"He dropped me off. He was headed into Beaver Creek to order some equipment."

"Was he, now?" The man settled on the stool next to him. "Well, we'll find out for sure soon enough."

"Why do I get the feeling none of you are Keith's friends?"

"We're concerned with his wellbeing. It amounts to the same thing, doesn't it?"

"Not really." He shoved his plate aside. "Thanks, Ted. I've got to run."

The suit stood up to block him, and Tanner heard the two guys in the booth get up as well. "Where are you off to? You said yourself, you got dropped off and haven't got any way back home. You stay and keep us company."

They all had guns. Tanner didn't need to see them to know it. He could take down this guy, but the other two were on the far side of the diner with a dozen customers between him and the door. He noticed Ted edging down the counter toward them and Walt and Martin Taylor shifting in their booth nearby. All right, if townsfolk had his back, Tanner would take the chance. "I don't think I will."

"I said sit down." The suit tried to force him back down on the stool.

Tried.

Instead of Tanner on the stool, the man found himself with his face slammed into the counter. "Haven't taken too kindly to orders from other people since I retired from the service."

The other two drew small automatics, but Ted, Walt and Martin had them down and disarmed in a heartbeat. "In case you couldn't tell"— Tanner thumped the guy against the counter again—"we don't like unfriendly strangers around here too much. Now, who sent you?"

"Fuck you."

"Too bad you're not my type." He jammed he knee into the guy's crotch, slamming his head down yet again. "Who sent you? Escavera?"

Still he didn't answer.

Good enough. "What about the other two, the ones who were going through town. Where are they?"

"Doing their job."

"Is this a retrieval or elimination?"

The guy stopped struggling. "That wasn't specified."

Which didn't bode well for Keith. He would be less trouble dead than alive.

CHAPTER 16

Keith pushed away from the desk and stretched. He had sent out eleven bids for new equipment, including new chutes, fencing and water tanks for the additional headstock Tanner wanted to add and a new baler, which would let them make better use of the grassland they had for winter feed. He had also ordered Tanner's Christmas presents. They hadn't really talked about Christmas, but Keith didn't care. He was looking forward to the look on Tanner's face when he opened the box of high-end sex toys. Keith would just have to make sure it wasn't in front of Marta.

Satisfied with the morning's work, and more than a little tired of being cooped up, he grabbed his coat to go for a walk.

Walk was a bit of a euphemism. It was nineteen degrees out, so he wasn't staying out long, but the fresh, cold air was invigorating, blowing all the cobwebs out of his brain as he made his way over to the paddock.

The other horses all trotted eagerly over to the fence on seeing him, hoping for their share of the sugar cubes and carrots Keith always brought with him, but to his surprise, Foster didn't join them. Instead, he paced the paddock from one end to the other again and again, pushing his shoulder against the end fence rails each time. Distracted, Keith offered the treats to the other animals, all the time watching the mongrel horse.

"Foster," he called, although the animal had never shown any response to the name. "Come on, boy. Carrot." He offered it out.

Clyde stole it out of his fingers.

"Damn it, Clyde!" Keith resisted the urge to smack him on the nose like an errant dog. Foster's agitation was starting to get to him as well. Keith went into the barn for some fresh water and some of the apples they kept in cold storage for the horses. Maybe if he went into the pen, Foster would calm down.

A car pulled up in the driveway. Keith heard the crunch of tires creeping over the stone parking area. Not truck tires, it wasn't heavy enough. So not Tanner.

Apple clutched in his hand, he peeked out the barn door.

The car was a late model Town Car, obviously a rental, although from the dust and salt on it, it had seen quite a few miles. The two men who got out had come even farther, judging by their dark suits and tans. And the automatics they slipped out of their coats to hold at the ready.

Foster screamed.

"Fucking horses," the taller of the two said. "It's the twenty-first century; what's the point?"

"They fetch good money if the stock is good. Just because your old man made you muck out the stalls while you were growing up..."

"Cars don't judge you."

Apparently they weren't trying to keep a low profile. Not a good sign. He crept closer to the edge of the barn door to get a clearer view.

Unlike the other horses that had backed off around the strangers, Foster kept close to the fence, watching the two men. Good to know someone had his back.

The keys were in the Land Rover. If he could just get to it, he might be able to get off the ranch without getting shot. Much.

The hired muscle was on the porch now, still in plain view of the Land Rover and the barn. Horse-Hater stepped to one side, while the other one knocked on the door. When no one answered, he knocked again before they began peering in the window.

Tanner's rifle was in the house.

Keith's brain was flying through his options in no sensible order. All he could focus on was that he needed to get out of here.

If he had his phone, he could alert Marta. And Tanner... Keith hoped he took his time in town. The Escavera men wouldn't blink at getting rid of an unneeded person.

None of which mattered. His phone was inside, next to the computer, charging. He was on his own.

Horse-Hater tried the door. Of course, Keith hadn't locked it. They never locked it. Keith wasn't even sure it actually had a lock. Horse-Hater turned to his partner. "Check the barn; I'll take the house."

Shit.

Keith gripped the apple harder as he withdrew farther into the shadows. A piece of fruit stood little chance against a semi-automatic, but it was better than nothing. The various farm implements around him might be useful, though they would force him into direct contact with Horse-Hater's buddy. His best chance would be to slip out unnoticed and avoid confrontation all together.

Foster screamed again, and Keith could hear him now slamming his body against the rails, making them clatter in their posts as he fought to escape. Keith knew the feeling. Although if he kept it up, Keith worried what the gunman would do to make him stop.

"Mr. Lewis, if you're in here, come on out. The less trouble you give us, the easier this will be all around."

Easier for him. Keith kept his mouth shut.

He could hide someplace, but anywhere he might hide would only trap him if he were found. If he got out the other end of the barn, he could try to make a run for the hills. Although the fields were all still deep in snow, so even if he did get away, he'd be easy to track. *Damn it.* Still, out of the barn was his best option for now.

He crept back through the horse boxes toward the stanchions for the cows. That was even more exposed without the safe walls of the stalls to duck behind. Keith's heart was pounding, making it hard to hear.

Foster shoved his head in the paddock door and blew at him, panicked. Keith nearly shrieked.

"These are some pretty horses, Mr. Lewis. Would be a shame for any of them to get hurt."

Thug Two's voice was closer now, calling in the door. There was a good hundred feet between Keith and the back door. There was no way he could sprint it without being seen. He did the only thing he could do. He squeezed himself behind the milk chiller and held his breath.

"It wasn't easy finding you. Those marshals get lucky sometimes. But the Escaveras always find their man. Only a matter of time...and a friendly tip."

Thug Two was in the barn now. Keith could hear him looking in each of the stalls. Keith fought not to panic.

"That's the problem with witness protection. Most times, the witnesses don't want to be protected. They don't want to give up their old life. They keep thinking someday they'll get to go back, and they want to make sure someone's waiting for them. So they make a mistake. They make a phone call. Just one. What can it hurt? And here we are."

Ryan had sold him out to the Escaveras. It was surprising in that it really wasn't. Ryan had always done anything to get ahead. Keith should have known better than to trust him.

Not his biggest problem at the moment, however. If he got out of this alive, then he'd worry about it.

Against all sanity, he inched along the wall behind the chiller closer to the gunman, hoping to slip out when they passed each other and make a break through the paddock to the Land Rover. He was almost to the end of the stalls now.

Keith reached out and slipped the bolt on the paddock door.

The gunman turned and smiled. "Told Jeremy you'd be in the barn."

Keith bolted out into the paddock, passing Foster.

He expected bullets to tear through his flesh any second.

Instead, he heard a scream. And it wasn't Foster this time.

Foster had charged past Keith into the barn and knocked the gunman to the ground, where he was now stomping on him with what could only be called feverish delight. The gun went off, but unaimed and useless under a thousand pounds of angry equine.

But the shot was enough to alert Horse-Hater, Jeremy, in the house.

Keith hid behind the other horses, a difficult challenge as they were now spooked and kept shifting around, looking for safety. There wasn't time to go back in the barn after Thug Two's gun, and Keith wouldn't have dared risk Foster's hooves anyway.

A moment later, neither mattered. Foster was back out in the paddock, blood flecked on his hooves and shaggy legs. He saw Jeremy as well, tracking him as he made his way across the parking area to the barn. It was eerie how aware the horse was, almost human. And angry.

As soon as Jeremy was out of the line of sight of the paddock, Foster nudged Keith and bent one knee. It was an easy sign to read— Get on.

Keith had barely gotten seated before Foster took off, leaving Keith no choice but to hold on tight and hope their luck held out.

With no saddle and no reins, Keith was entirely at Foster's behest. But the horse had had the best sense of the two of them through the whole debacle, so Keith knit his fingers into Foster's shaggy mane as they vaulted the fence and landed with a jolt in the parking area.

Foster didn't hesitate, his feet already flying across the gravel toward the open field west of the house. There was a shout behind them, followed by three sharp cracks that made Keith flinch. They were already streaking out onto the prairie when Keith heard an engine behind him.

"Keep going, boy. We've made it this far."

Foster didn't need his instruction or encouragement.

They slowed as they crested a hill half a mile from the house. Keith looked back, but the house and surrounding area looked as they should, empty of all but a beat-up red Ford truck and the Land Rover. Jeremy must have decided to cut his losses and taken off. Still, Keith wasn't ready to take any chances.

Instead, he tugged on Foster's mane to turn him in the general direction of the main road. "Come on, boy. Let's go keep an eye out for the cavalry."

Foster obeyed without question.

Out of the protection of the barn, the wind cut through Keith's jeans and barn coat, making him miss his ugly, unfashionable quilted overalls all the more, grateful for the little warmth Foster put out. Their path mirrored the circuit Keith and Tanner had made of the fences their first day out riding, except Keith kept away from the driveway. The rough terrain was all that stood between him and Jeremy's backup, assuming there was more than what Foster had pounded into the barn floor. As long as he could see the drive, he was happy. He'd be happier when he could see the road, though.

It took almost an hour to get to the high rise near where the driveway let out onto the road. The gate stood open, drifting back and forth in the cold Montana wind. Keith could hear it clang against the post occasionally even at this distance. The road back to Jensen's Crossing was empty and black, barely curving as wisps of snow drifted across the white and yellow lines. He'd be able to see anyone, friend or foe, coming long before they got close.

He was tempted to get down off Foster's back and hunker down against him to get out of the wind, but he needed the extra height to keep watch. For his part, Foster was a rock, stiff-legged and attentive despite the grass poking temptingly out of the snow. For a minute, Keith felt like an old Indian scout, watching the horizon for the coming enemy. The thought passed quickly until all he felt was cold.

Finally, he spied movement in the distance. Vehicles, approaching fast.

He heard the sirens before he could make out the flashing lights. But more of a relief was the black F-150 racing ahead of the two police cars.

"There's the cavalry, Foster. Let's go meet them, huh?"

Foster seemed to nod in agreement before setting off.

The vehicles pulled off onto the side of the road as Keith and Foster approached.

Tanner jumped out of the truck when they started picking their way down the slope. He was already through the wire fence by the time they reached the bottom and yanked Keith down unceremoniously. "Are you okay? Did they hurt you?"

"I'm fine." Just that quickly, he was safe again. "I'm freezing my nuts off, but I'm fine."

"How'd you get away?"

"Had a bit of help from a good friend." Grinning, he patted Foster's flank. "But how did you know I was in trouble?"

"There were three more in town. I guess, with so much area to cover, they figured they needed to spread out to find you."

Now that the immediate relief of being safe had passed, Keith decided he should be upfront. "My ex, Ryan, sold me out." Before Tanner could respond, he added, "But it's my own fault. I called him a while back when I was feeling low and let it slip about being in Montana."

Tanner's jaw clenched. "Marta's on her way. You'll have to tell her. If that's true, your friend is in big trouble."

"I don't care. Right now, I just want to get warm."

Tanner relaxed a little. "Come on. Let's get you home. Lloyd," he called to the sheriff waiting on the other side of the fence, "you got any rope in the car? I need to improvise a halter."

"Yeah, let me get it."

Keith caught Tanner's arm. "There's another problem. Unless Jeremy grew a conscience, there's a dead body in the barn."

"A...what? Who the hell's Jeremy?"

"One of the two Escavera men who isn't currently a bloody mess inside the stables. At least that's what the dead guy called him."

"Christ. Lloyd, I think this is more your department than mine," Tanner said, taking the rope from the returned sheriff.

"What's that?"

Keith told the whole story, standing out there on the side of the road in the icy wind. There wasn't any point in putting it off. Tanner and

Sheriff Wahl listened attentively without asking any questions until Keith got to the end.

"All right, son, I'm going to need to see this body."

"Yeah, go on ahead. Foster and I will follow you in."

Tanner stopped him. "You don't have to ride. I can tie the horse behind the truck and lead him back."

"He and I started this thing together; I think we need to finish it together, don't you?" He reached over to scratch between Foster's shaggy ears.

Foster bobbed his head, then bent down to nudge at Keith's pocket. Reaching in, Keith found a withered apple he had put there hours before. He offered it to Foster, who took it with delicate lips.

"That's eerie," Tanner said.

Keith chuckled. "No, that's Foster."

Once he finished the apple, Foster nosed Keith's shoulder.

"Good idea, let's get this over with."

"Eerie," Tanner repeated, but there was no mistaking the pleased smile touching his lips.

Things could have turned out a lot worse.

*   *   *

Marta pulled into the drive at eleven.

Keith and Tanner both sat at the dining room table. Her arrival wasn't a surprise, but they were both on edge anyway when they heard the SUV in the drive. Tanner picked up the rifle leaning against the wall behind him and went to check through the front door sidelight window. The parking area was brightly lit. Tanner had switched the floods from motion detecting to on, and the brilliant halogen light obliterated the night sky and the outlines of the hills around the house. Keith didn't relax until he saw Tanner put down the rifle and unlock the door.

Marta didn't even say hello as she walked through the door. "We've got an early morning flight. If your things aren't packed, pack them now."

"Now?" Keith had known he wouldn't get to stay, but he had figured to get a little time. "We won't even get to Great Falls until two in the morning at this point."

"We aren't going to Great Falls. I've got a private plane waiting in Lewistown. You've got two minutes."

He'd earned the wrath of Marta, deservedly so, but still... Pushing out of his chair, he headed into his bedroom. He ignored the heated conversation going on in the dining room as he began stuffing his duffle bag with the clothes he'd brought with him. There wasn't any reason to take the clothes he'd gotten for the farm.

He was shoving the last of his jeans into his bag when the argument finally quieted. Looking up, he wasn't surprised to find Tanner standing in the door. "Hope the next guy is close to my size. Seems a shame for these clothes to go to waste."

"Take the boots. They're shaped to your foot now. No use to anyone else."

Keith was leaving here with cowboy boots. Jesus, who was he anymore?

If he'd kept his damned mouth shut, he wouldn't be wondering. Things had been good. Fucking Ryan. *No, fucking you, Keith, for screwing things up.*

Keith grabbed up the boots and his bag. "I'm ready."

Tanner studied him a long moment before crossing the room, catching Keith by his shirtfront and jerking him into a ferocious kiss.

Keith dropped bag and boots with a thud to wrap his arms around Tanner, desperate for this one last contact. He had never let himself think about it before, but now he was being forced to leave, he knew the only place he ever wanted to be was here with Tanner.

"Are you about read— Damn!"

Marta was in the hall, back turned politely. Keith had never seen her embarrassed before.

"Give us a minute," Tanner snapped.

"I can't. That plane's not going to wait all night, and we have to get to Denver in time for his next flight. We have to go now, Tanner."

Keith took the initiative and stepped away. The quicker he left, the less it would hurt.

Bullshit.

"It's been an experience," was all he trusted himself to say as he retrieved his things and walked out of the bedroom and toward the door.

Keith didn't even bother with his jacket, just kept moving until he was outside and settled in the Cherokee. Marta soon emerged, but not Tanner. *Better that way.*

Marta climbed into the vehicle. "Keith, I—"

"I only have myself to blame, Marta. Leave it and get me on that goddamned plane."

For a minute, he thought she was going to argue with him. Instead, she stuck the key in the ignition and started the car.

The floodlights dimmed as they pulled out of the drive. Act two over, Keith thought. Now for a brief intermission while the actors rearrange the set.

Damn it.

CHAPTER 17

Tanner had gotten along fine by himself for all the years he'd worked the ranch. An extra pair of hands was nice, but he didn't *need* it. However, since Keith had left— No, not going there. When winter was over, things would turn around. The endless cold and snow and bleakness affected even him. Spring would be here soon enough and then he'd be too busy to think.

He liked that a lot.

Grabbing his coat, he went outside and over to check on the horses.

Foster ran up to the gate as he approached, eagerly looking for Keith. Nearly four months, and he wouldn't give up.

"He's not coming, you stupid animal," Tanner chided, tossing a flake of hay over the fence. "Get used to it."

Foster ignored the hay to keep watch, the other horses eating it all while he scanned the horizon.

Tanner shook his head and went in to milk the cows.

He'd have to get someone else in to do this in a few weeks. The cows were due to start dropping calves then, and that would go on until the beginning of June. He'd be spending those six weeks in the saddle, helping the mothers in trouble, pulling lanky calves out of gullies, fending off opportunistic coyotes and eating dried beef and canned beans. He wouldn't have the time to milk, let alone the energy. He could ask Cecily, but it was too far a haul for her to come out twice a day. Maybe Derek could recommend some kid looking for a short-term job. Hell, they could live at the house. It wasn't like he was going to be there.

He'd tried not be there since Keith left.

The equipment orders Keith had been working on when he'd left sat unplaced. This year's expansion was on hold. Tanner hadn't realized how much of the plans they'd made had been with the thought that Keith would be a part of it. It hadn't been intentional. Neither of them had discussed it, but in the back of his mind, Tanner had always seen Keith picking up the slack during calving, helping with the new pastures, just being a part of ranch life. Of Tanner's life. Even four months on, he couldn't let go of that.

"I'm as bad as the damn horse."

The cow he was milking turned her head to look at him, placid and uncomprehending.

"Yeah, I know, I did it to myself. Now mind your own damned business."

The cow blinked and kept watching him.

"And I'm talking to a cow. Fantastic."

Finishing up, he put out some grain and went to muck out the stalls.

It didn't take nearly enough time.

Foster had started nibbling at the hay when Tanner emerged, but still had most of his attention on the horizon.

Tanner's landline was ringing when he got inside. He let the answering machine get it.

"Tanner, it's too fucking early in the morning. I know you're up, so answer the damned phone."

Marta, cheerful as ever.

He did. "Okay, I know you're on the west coast."

"How?"

"It's eight-thirty. If you were on the east coast, you'd be yelling at me for sleeping late."

"Good to see you're as smart as ever," she said dryly.

"Would you like to call me back *after* you've had your third cup of coffee?"

"Don't be an ass." She continued, "I thought you'd want to know the Escavera verdict came down. The bastard won't see the light of day anytime soon."

"Oh." It meant Keith was finally safe. At least as safe as he ever would be now. And free to go where he wanted, so long as it wasn't Texas. "That's good."

Tanner could almost hear her rolling her eyes. "That's good. Don't you even want to know where Keith is?"

"Where is he?"

"When I talked to him last night, he was in Baltimore."

Baltimore. The wheels in Tanner's head started turning.

"Oh, and I sent you back your coffee cup."

"My what?"

"Your mug. Remember? You threatened me if I didn't get it back to you? Well, it should get there today. Let me know if it doesn't."

"Marta, it's just a damn piece of secondhand kitchenware."

"Let me know, all right? You may not care, but I do."

"Fine. If it doesn't get here today, I'll let you know." It would take him a day or so to make arrangements, anyway.

"I'll be checking in."

"It was months ago, Marta. I'd honestly forgotten about it."

"Sounds like someone else is behind on their caffeine consumption."

Tanner sighed. "I'll call. Now, can I go?" It was a stupid secondhand mug. If she were so worried about it, she should have kept it.

"No one ever wants to talk these days."

"Goodbye, Marta."

"'Bye, cowboy."

As soon as he got off the phone, he pulled out his laptop. A quick Internet search told him was too late to go now, but there was a flight out of Great Falls at nine in the morning that would have him in Baltimore by one-thirty with only one stop. Without stopping to argue with himself, he bought the ticket. Yes, it was stupid and impulsive. It didn't matter. Once he got there, he'd call and badger Marta for more details. She'd give in eventually.

His normally calm, routine day was thrown into a frenzy. He couldn't just take off. There were arrangements to be made for the animals, and he had to get word out to the guys on calf watch that he was going to be out of town for God knew how long. Maybe forever. He didn't care. He'd learn to love the city if it meant getting to be with Keith.

Around three, he heard tires crunching on the gravel drive. Why Marta would waste good money on a stupid mug... But his cousin always was a bit odd.

He finished typing up the email he was working on before getting up to answer the door.

"I'm sorry you had to come all the way out here for—"

Keith grinned and held out a brown box taped within an inch of its life. "Marta decided she didn't trust FedEx."

Tanner knocked the box out of Keith's hand and pulled him into his arms.

"If you broke it after all the trouble I went through..." But he wrapped his arms tightly around Tanner, nose cold against Tanner's neck. "I have missed you."

When Tanner kissed him, it was like they had never been apart. Keith still tasted as he always had, faintly minty, distinctly coffee-y and with a savory, salty undertone all his own. Keith was as hungry for it as Tanner was, opening his mouth under Tanner's demanding probe. It took a while, but eventually Tanner had to breathe. "Foster missed you."

"Foster, huh?"

"He's been looking for you every morning since you left."

"I hope it kept him out of trouble. I'd hate for him to have turned into a serial killer while I was gone."

"He's been pretty docile, actually. Of course, now you're back, there's no telling what trouble he'll get up to."

"What trouble *he'll* get up to?"

Tanner fixed Keith with a look. "Fine, both Foster and I have missed you and have been bored out of our minds since you left. Happy?"

"Not really."

Tanner pulled back. "No?"

Keith shook his head. "Right now there's only one thing that can really make me happy."

"What's that?"

"For you to tell me I can come home."

"Bit late for that," Tanner said with a smile. "But seeing as you're already here, you'd damn well better not be leaving again."

"Even Marta couldn't drag me away."

"I think she wants you here as much as I do."

"Oh?"

"She didn't tell me you were coming."

Keith frowned in thought. "Yeah, sounds like Marta. Matchmaking again."

"Well, her matchmaking days are over. At least with me. She can turn her wiles on Billy and the rest of our cousins." Tanner hauled

Keith close, breathing him in and just savoring the feel of him, then finally released him. "Go give Foster some attention. I've gotta ring Marta and tell her my mug arrived."

Keith wasn't so compliant. "Foster can wait." He shoved Tanner back toward the door. "And so can Marta."

Tanner would have been a fool to argue. Unable to stop smiling, he dragged Keith inside. Four months. Yeah, everyone else could wait.

BLOOD ON THE MOUNTAIN

WATCH MY BACK

CHAPTER 1

Gabe Callan barreled through the front door of Callan Securities, twenty-five minutes late and already in a foul mood.

The waiting room was empty. *Damn.*

"Ms. Murray—" Hettie began, but recoiled behind the reception desk at the ferocious glare he shot her. He'd lost a major potential client because of the vagaries of the Chicago L; he didn't need the blow-by-blow from her.

In the hall, Jeannie caught him before he could slam into his office. "Calm down." Her voice was low and even, the hands on his chest soothing, but determined. "You don't want to make a scene in front of the new client."

"What are you talking about? He's—"

"In the conference room with a coffee, the new client brochure and the pitch video. When you were late, I got things started without you. Did you forget to charge your phone again?"

"God damn CTA. I would have been fine if they weren't doing track work on the Green Line. We stood for fifteen minutes at Conservatory before they finally let us through. I don't know why I don't just drive."

"Because if you did, you'd have been stuck even longer in traffic." She straightened his tie and took his briefcase. "You got it now?"

He took a deep breath and blew it out before smiling wryly. "Yeah, I got it. I should have known you'd have it covered. Why did I ever divorce you?"

"Because our sex life sucked." Her answering grin was playful. It had taken a while to get to that point, though. The fact that she had walked in on him being fucked by her cousin Marcus might've had something to do with that.

"Not entirely. There were moments."

"Moments, yes. But moments aren't enough when a girl lacks certain equipment. Though I will say my fantasies are much more entertaining now." Jeannie gave him a not so gentle shove. "Now get your ass to work."

"Yes'm." Saluting her, Gabe made his way to the conference room.

He was lucky to still have Jeannie in his life at all. She could have taken the house and the business when his sexual identity crisis had ended their marriage. Instead, she'd sat him down, had a long talk with him, gone to counseling with him and when they had divorced, it had been amicable, leaving her free to find someone who could give her everything Gabe couldn't. She had kept her share of the business, though. Considering the current international climate, that had probably been a smart decision.

Gabe rapped on the door before letting himself into the conference room.

Their new potential client, Nathan Graves, greeted him with a smile. "I see you survived the travails of Chicago public transport. Your partner wasn't optimistic."

"I apologize for being late. The L is usually reliable until you rely on it." He offered his hand. "Gabriel Callan. It's a pleasure to meet you, Mr. Graves."

"Nathan, please." His grip was strong and sure and his lingering smile crinkled the corners of his blue eyes. While his salt and pepper hair was cut roughly to accentuate strong features, he didn't seem vain enough about it that he bothered to color out the gray. Gabe liked him already. "Don't worry about it. Baltimore's isn't much better, and we only have one line."

"Less to go wrong that way, at least."

"Yeah, but when it's down, everyone's screwed."

Smiling, Gabe pulled out a chair across from Nathan at the table and sat. "So what is it you're looking for from us? I'm not underestimating the dangers of South America, but it does tend to be more business friendly than the Middle East."

"How much do you know about Niche Habitat?"

"I read your prospectus. Interesting project. Affordable, self-sustainable microhousing. Innovative."

"We hope it will be more than innovative." Nathan's dark eyes danced as he relaxed in his chair. "There are too many places in the world plagued by substandard housing and limited to nonexistent utilities. Niche Habitat wants to provide that housing at a fraction of the cost of traditional construction. Our hope is that by improving the basic standard of living in urban slums, in war-ravaged areas or even just rural areas in the developing world, we'll be able to help change the broader social dynamic as well.

"People who aren't dependent on drug lords for their cooking fuel or at the whim of tribal rivalries for their electricity should be better able to speak up for themselves and build stronger, healthier governments."

"Sounds like benevolent regime change."

"By invitation only. Which is where you come in." Nathan leaned forward. The man was a skilled speaker, Gabe had to give him credit where credit was due. "We've been invited to help convert a *favela,* a slum neighborhood in the heart of Rio de Janiero, into a fully autonomous community based on Niche Habitat's philosophy. The Babilonia neighborhood was taken over by the government in 2009. It overlooks two of the richest beaches in the city and, with the Olympics coming, the local government wants to get rid of what it sees as an eyesore, a blight on the region.

"Rather than gentrifying it, we've convinced them to let us come in, work with the *Moradores da favela,* the local residents, to rebuild without the influence of the drug gangs that had run the place. But as you can imagine, not everyone's happy about the idea."

"Topmost being said drug lords," Gabe said.

"Exactly."

"What are you looking for as far as security? If we did job site protection, we would probably contract with locals for that—"

"Nothing that major yet," Nathan interrupted. "The whole project is still in the development stage. I need to go to Rio for a few weeks to meet with local government, representatives from the neighborhood, start generating interest in the whole project. If the community's not behind us, then nothing we do will improve things for them. I need a personal bodyguard for the trip, someone to watch my back while I'm pressing flesh."

Gabe wouldn't mind either of those things.

He mentally berated himself for the thought. Bad form and very unprofessional. A voice not unlike Jeannie's chimed in to say that it had been way too long since he last got laid. Business was business and private pursuits lay elsewhere. The divorce had taught him that if nothing else.

"Everything all right?" Nathan asked, and Gabe realized he'd been quiet for far too long.

"Yeah, just doing a quick run through of who'd be right for the job."

"Whoever it is, I don't want an ape in a dark suit. I need someone who can look non-threatening and serious at the same time. That's the reason I've come to you. If I wanted killers, I could go to Blackwater, or whatever they're called now, or one of those other mercenary-inspired companies. You have a reputation for ethics. That's what I'm looking for."

"That's the main reason I set up this business. Unfortunately, not everyone appreciates it."

"Try running a non-profit some time."

"I think I'd rather have people shooting at me."

Nathan grinned. "If this goes well, you might get your wish. We're hoping to go into Iraq and Afghanistan next."

"I look forward to that. We shouldn't have any trouble getting a secure car by next week. Not a Hummer," he added before Nathan could protest, "and not black. As far as the bodyguard goes I've got a couple of guys in mind who would work with your specs. Unless you'd rather have a woman?"

Nathan seemed to give it serious consideration, but eventually shook his head. "In such a macho country, no one would see her as a deterrent, even after she'd killed a couple of men. Hell, it might make us more of a target."

"Good, then we're on the same page. I'm going to have Jeannie come in and get your itinerary and details. We'll make all your travel arrangements and hotel bookings to ensure your security." Gabe stood, his part in the transaction concluded.

Just as Gabe reached the door, Nathan asked, "What about you?"

"What about me?"

"You just the boss here, or do you get your hands dirty from time to time?"

Maybe it was wishful thinking, but Nathan's look seemed to convey more than professional interest.

"We don't all have the good fortune to be able to go out in the field," Gabe apologized. "Don't worry. I'd trust my life with any of my guys. You'll be perfectly safe."

"I wasn't worried about my safety." The tone was unmistakable.

Maybe it wasn't wishful thinking after all.

All the more reason not to get personally involved. "I'll send Jeannie in." Gabe managed to not embarrass himself. "It was good to meet you, Mr. Graves."

"You, too, Gabriel. I look forward to seeing you again soon."

He got out of the room with a brusque handshake and the shreds of his dignity. He didn't fool Jeannie, though, who was waiting just down the hall. "What's the matter with you?"

"Nothing. I'm fine. Go fill out the itinerary forms with Graves, will you?"

She frowned, watching him a moment longer. "All right. But something's going on, and you're going to tell me."

"I always do." And he ducked in the relative safety of his office, closing the door behind him.

*   *   *

Jeannie let him stew until the end of the day. "Spill," she ordered, perching on the edge of his desk.

"There's nothing to spill, Jeannie. Let it go."

"I don't think so. I've never seen you come out of a meeting like that. What did he say to you?"

Gabe refused to look away from his monitor. "Nothing. He didn't say anything."

Jeannie crossed her arms, and he could feel her eyes boring into him. "He's not bad looking," she said meaningfully.

Gabe closed his eyes. "Jeannie—"

"Not too broad in the chest, mind you, but he has a very nice ass."

"I didn't notice his ass. He didn't get out of the chair long enough." *So much for that ruse.*

"But you noticed the rest."

"Don't, Jeannie."

"He asked me if you're single."

"Christ, Jeannie, you didn't—"

"I told him that signs point to yes, but he'd be better off asking you directly."

Gabe wasn't remotely grateful that his fifteenth-story windows did not open. Jumping surely had to be less painful than this.

The only response was to change the subject entirely. Or as much as possible. "I think Timson would be a good fit. And he's got a passing familiarity with Portuguese."

"Passing, but yours is better." She leaned in. "And you've had more experience with cartel politics than Timson."

"What about—"

"McGreggor's still in Columbia, and likely to be through the end of the year. Unless he gets himself or the client killed."

"Which he won't."

"Which he won't," she agreed. "So that leaves you."

"Or you."

Jeannie snorted. "Sweetie, I work management for a reason. Fieldwork was fun, but I don't miss it *that* much. And, if you've forgotten, I'm a girl. No one wants to make a tough job tougher."

He'd said as much to Nathan in their meeting.

Time for another tactic. "I can't leave the office. We're walking a fine edge right now. I need to—"

"Why are you so scared of this guy?" She eyed him with the patented Jeannie Murray stare that had reduced lesser men to quivering fools. "Because he finds you attractive?"

If she was already breaking out the hard stare, there was only one course of action. The truth. "Because I find *him* attractive," Gabe admitted. "Which is bad in our line of work."

"Bullshit."

"It affects your judgment."

"Coward."

"Jeannie!"

She didn't relent. "You last got laid, when...four months ago?"

"Keeping track of my social life?"

"It's good for morale. Come on, Gabe, this is a cakewalk, and you know it. You're going to Rio, for God's sake! The home of nude beaches and those fruity drinks with umbrellas in them. And you're going with a good-looking man your own age who thinks you're as sexy as I do."

"I'm not going, Jeannie."

"The hell you aren't. I'm the dispatcher, remember? And I say you are the best person to take this assignment." Then to add the final nail, she said, "If you think for one minute I can't handle this business for two weeks without you..."

"That's not what this is about!"

"Then you're going. Discussion closed." She leaned in to drape her arms around his neck affectionately. "Don't you want something better than casual hookups with club junkies?"

He sighed. "One, you know I like brains to go with the body, so of course. And two, it's not good for business."

"How is it *bad* for business? If you want his ass, aren't you going to be all the more invested in making sure you protect it?"

He glowered at her. "There are days I think it would have been easier if we'd stayed married."

Jeannie kissed his temple before backing off. "Yeah, but it wouldn't have been half as much fun."

"For you, maybe." With a sigh, he slouched back in his chair. "It's bad for business because he has a bigger contract for us in the future if this goes well. The best way to ruin that is to have a relationship with him go bad."

"Then you have even more incentive to make it succeed." Heading for the door, she smirked over her shoulder. "Don't forget our first time was when we were supposed to be watching each other's backs. And look how well that turned out."

CHAPTER 2

Nathan hated fundraisers, but not as much as he hated black-tie ones. Tugging said tie a little looser, he picked up his drink and scanned the room. These to-dos were necessary evils. He couldn't wait to get down to Brazil, where he could justifiably ignore this end of the business for a while.

"It wouldn't kill you to smile, you know," a low voice spoke from beside him.

"I'll smile when I can get out of this damn suit." Although his companion had already lifted his mood somewhat.

"Is that an invitation?"

Terry Graham had been Nathan's assistant since before Niche Habitat had even been formed. He knew all of Nathan's secrets and knew there was no way Nathan would ever hit on him. Nathan needed him too much. Besides, Terry's girlfriend didn't share well. "You wish."

Terry grinned and adjusted Nathan's tie. "Just relax. As soon as you give the pitch, we're out of here."

"These things irritate the shit out of me. The money spent by one table of these 'donors' could pay for one of our units, complete with furniture. They just want their pound of flesh first."

"Yeah, but their pound of flesh is a serving of rubber chicken that's probably crawling with salmonella."

"Now you know why I spend so much time at the bar. Alcohol counteracts many ills."

Terry shook his head and flagged down the bartender. "How did the security meeting go this morning?"

"Promising."

"Oh?"

Nathan chuckled.

"That sounds ominous."

"Let's just say the view was definitely worth the three-hour flight to O'Hare."

Terry gave him a suspicious look. "I never knew you to get sentimental about a place."

"Oh, I wasn't talking about Chicago."

Terry rolled his eyes. "You are trouble."

"I hope so."

Folding his arms, Terry waited. "Are you going to make me drag the details from you?"

"Could be fun."

"Nathan."

"Does Anna know you live out your homosexual fantasies vicariously through me?"

"Nathan, if I wanted to live out my homosexual fantasies, it wouldn't be vicariously."

With a grin, Nathan relented. "His name is Gabriel Callan, and he's the head of Callan Securities. Good-looking, fit and, according to his business partner, unattached."

"You asked—of course, you asked. Who am I talking to?" But Terry was amused. "I assume you requested the fine Mr. Callan as your personal guard."

"Naturally."

"You aren't that big a fish, Nathan. I doubt the president of the company is going to run away with you for two weeks just because you're hot for him."

"Maybe not. But it doesn't hurt to ask."

Before Terry could comment further, a broad-shouldered man with receding hair halfway between blond and white approached them. "Nathan Graves?"

Was "hello" too much to ask? "Yes?"

The man held out his hand. "Peter Deguerre. I was hoping we might have a word."

Taking the cue, but looking none too pleased, Terry said, "There's Anna. I'll talk to you later."

Once they were alone, Nathan inquired, "What can I do for you, Mr. Deguerre?"

"It's what I can do for you."

"Oh? And what's that?"

Deguerre offered his card. It was black with silver lettering, an embossed dagger on one side. "I understand you had a meeting with Gabe Callan this morning."

"How did you hear about that?"

Deguerre shrugged. "It's what I do. Or, more importantly, it's what I could be doing for you."

"Which you still haven't told me." Although Nathan had a pretty good idea.

"The last place you want less than the best, particularly security wise, is in Rio."

"Is that so?"

"Don't get me wrong. I've worked with Gabe. He's a good man, *was* a good agent. But his field experience was limited to domestic security. He doesn't know the international situation as well as others."

"Like yourself."

Deguerre nodded toward the card in Nathan's hand. "Dagger Security is experienced in combat zones, Mr. Graves. We've got government contracts second only to Xe Services—"

"Formerly Blackwater."

Deguerre brushed the clarification aside. "We know the field, Mr. Graves. Why not let us put that know-how to work for you?"

"Not to be rude, Mr. Deguerre, but Niche Habitat is a small-scale nonprofit. What could you possible want with a contract with us?"

"You're too modest, Mr. Graves. We've seen your technology, and there's great potential for it in some of the markets we serve."

If the man called him Mr. Graves one more time, Nathan was going to punch him in the neck. "Which still wouldn't impact your bottom line. A security contract with us, even in the heart of a combat zone, would be a pittance compared to what you'd get from your government contracts." He paused a moment before calling Deguerre out. "So what is this really about?"

If Nathan hadn't been looking for it, he would have missed the subtle twitch of Deguerre's eyes. "Sometimes it's not about the money. It's about doing the right thing."

Instead of laughing in the man's face, like he was tempted to do, Nathan asked, "You say you used to work with Gabriel Callan?"

Deguerre's jaw tightened. "We graduated from Quantico together."

"But you didn't work together."

"We crossed paths...a few times."

Likely butted heads as well.

Nathan held the card out to Deguerre. "I appreciate your interest. However, Callan Securities really is the better fit for my company."

"Mr. Graves, you really should consider all your options. Rio is a dangerous place right now."

Nathan made a small, rehearsed gesture he knew Terry could read from across the room. "A situation of which I'm well aware. It's why I hired a security firm in the first place." On cue, his phone rang. "Excuse me. I need to take this." Putting the phone to his ear, he pointedly turned his back on Deguerre.

"Problems?" Terry asked.

"I understand. No, of course, we'd be happy to review the contract with you."

"Relax, he just left. Didn't look too happy, though. What was that all about?"

"Rival security firm to Callan. Maybe a rival to Gabe Callan himself. He knew a bit too much about the whole thing to make me comfortable."

"You going to tell Callan about it?"

"No real reason to, unless Deguerre is persistent."

"He seems the type, and not in the way you prefer."

Terry's humor dissipated some of Nathan's residual tension from the conversation with Deguerre. "Thanks again."

"What kind of assistant would I be if I'd let you suffer much longer?"

"You'd be a better assistant, not to mention friend, if you hadn't abandoned me in the first place. Especially since Anna isn't even here."

"You know that and I know that. But our friend Deguerre didn't. Sometimes you have to play the game to see what people are after."

"True, but I'd make an exception in his case."

"Want me to see what I can find out about him?"

"And Dagger Security. It seems weird he'd push so hard on this for a personal grudge."

"I don't know. It's amazing the lengths people will go to for something like that." Nathan didn't need to see his friend to know Terry was frowning. "You may still want to give Callan a head's up just to be safe."

"I'll keep it in mind. Thanks again."

While an excuse to call Gabe would be nice, somehow he didn't think the man would take it well to hear someone had been poaching his business, especially if there really was a rivalry between the two men. And there was the added complication of how Deguerre had gotten his information in the first place. Either someone in Gabe's organization had a big mouth, or someone in Nathan's did.

With Terry looking into things, all Nathan needed to do was keep his eyes open and get through the next week until he was on the way to Rio.

CHAPTER 3

They met at Hartsfield Airport in Atlanta to make the connection for a shared flight to Brazil. Gabe had thought about having Nathan fly to Chicago and take a direct flight from there, but that would be overplaying the security a bit. If he was safe enough to fly to Chicago, he was safe enough to fly to Atlanta, and this way Gabe wasn't adding an extra three hours to his client's already long flight itinerary.

Gabe felt overdressed in his simple business suit compared to Nathan's jeans and polo, but habits of the Bureau died hard. When you were on the clock, you dressed the part, even if it didn't make the most sense.

"You might feel better if you at least ditched the tie," Nathan suggested, as if reading his mind.

"I don't want you to doubt you're getting what you paid for."

"I'm just glad you could rearrange your schedule to handle me personally."

Gabe didn't wince at the thought of handling Nathan. "You had some pretty specific requirements, and we wanted to be sure you were happy with the service. Our best man for this kind of work was on another assignment, so it just seemed right for me to take it on. And Jeannie thinks I need to get out more. In the field," he hastily added.

"There are worse places than Rio to work, that's for certain." Nathan's eyes trailed, with unmistakable intent, over him. "You look like you could use some sun and fun. Though, no fear, you'll be doing plenty of work, too."

"I'm more of a mountains guy than fun in the sun." He checked their flight information and started toward their concourse.

"You like to be active." Nathan said it like he knew it already. "Not that into lying around doing nothing."

"Not really."

"I get that. But sometimes it's good to let go and just lie back."

The thought was enough to make Gabe's skin itch. "Doing nothing has never gone well for me."

"Maybe you haven't been doing it right."

"I'll keep that in mind if someone takes a shot at you."

Nathan chuckled. "Okay, you win. Feel free to be as proactive as you like if anyone tries to kill me."

"And if they don't?"

"Enjoy yourself. If you can."

Oh, Gabe could. That was what he was afraid of.

Forty-five minutes later, they were strapped into their respective business class seats and the plane was taxiing for takeoff.

The flight was nine hours, and Gabe was glad Nathan had chosen to sit in the window seat instead of the aisle. The thought of being trapped in one place that long made him queasy. When Nathan pulled out a book, Gabe asked, "Do you mind if I go to sleep for a while?"

Nathan's lips quirked. "I suppose I can manage to stay out of trouble."

"Smartass."

Gabe reclined his seat, grateful for the few scant inches gained by flying business over economy.

He fell into a light sleep, lulled by the hum of the plane's engines. Even before the Bureau, he'd been able to rest without losing complete awareness of surroundings. Of course, being the youngest of three might have had more to do with that than any innate ability. Surviving sibling pranks did wonders for one's self-preservation.

He slept through the first drink service, but woke up when the lunch cart came through. Nathan seemed to have made good progress on his book, which was propped open in his lap as he dozed.

Gabe took advantage of the opportunity to study the man.

Physically, he hit all the right buttons. Toned more than fit, with abundant laugh lines and a mouth made for smiling...and other more salacious things. He was also several inches shorter than Gabe, which was a particular attraction that Gabe didn't want to admit to.

He shifted uncomfortably in his seat. He really shouldn't be thinking about a client like that, even if Nathan had shown obvious signs of being interested. It wasn't professional. If they did get in trouble, it was a good way to get one or both of them killed.

"Keep thinking so hard and you're going to get grooves in your forehead," Nathan said without opening his eyes.

So much for subtlety. "You're supposed to be asleep."

"No, *you're* supposed to be asleep. I'm supposed to be reading." Nathan cracked one eye open. "What are you so afraid of?"

"It's not fear; it's professionalism."

Nathan snorted. "This is new for you, isn't it?"

Gabe was grateful when Nathan closed his eye again. "About a year-and-a-half."

"Jeannie took it well."

"Jeannie was a fucking saint."

"Jeannie's also got balls." The corners of his mouth lifted. "If she were my type, she'd probably be where you are now."

"You could do worse."

"So why isn't she? Where you are now, I mean."

"She had enough of fieldwork in the agency. She prefers working with people rather than strategies. And she's a she, and we all agreed that's not the best choice for where we're going."

Now both eyes were open and fixed on him. "Is that all I am to you then, Gabe? A strategy?"

"It's what you hired me for."

"Fair enough." Nathan turned his attention back to his book.

Gabe waited. "That's it?"

"You're not interested in anything beyond business. I get that."

"Hey, now, I never said I wasn't—" Gabe caught himself, but it was already too late. It appeared Nathan was every bit as skilled as Jeannie at getting Gabe to play into his hand. That didn't bode well at all.

Nathan grinned. "Now we're getting somewhere."

"I thought you were supposed to be one of the good guys."

"I'm *very* good." He picked up his book again. "Doesn't mean I'm a pussy cat."

"Maybe after all of this…" Gabe attempted to go for the middle ground.

Nathan wasn't having it. "A lot can happen between now and then. Believe it or not, you can mix business with pleasure and not have it blow up in your face."

"Tell that to Jeannie."

"Seeing as Jeannie was quite encouraging, I think your opinion differs from hers on the matter. And she doesn't strike me as the type to risk a client for petty revenge."

"I don't need her to set me up with dates."

"I'm not a date. I'm a client."

"And that's why this is a problem."

"Pretty big assumption that there even is a 'this.'"

Gabe glared at Nathan. "You're trying to drive me crazy, aren't you?"

"Depends. Is it working?"

As if lying would help. "Yes. Now read your damned book."

CHAPTER 4

Two woefully inadequate meals and a three-hour nap later, Nathan waited anxiously for the cabin door to open. It must have been worse for Gabe, who had already stated his preference of being active. By the end of the flight, he had been like a caged animal, pacing up and down the aisle as though looking for an escape.

But soon they were out and heading away from the gate and toward the main concourse, carry-ons in hand.

"You didn't check anything, did you?" Gabe asked, sounding as if there were no greater social faux pas.

"Is it a deal breaker if I did?"

That earned Nathan a flickering hint of a smile. "It might be."

"In that case, no, I didn't." Then he added, "I've also had really bad luck with baggage claim. Better to pack what I need so it's with me instead of taking my chances."

Gabe eyed Nathan's bag suspiciously. "How did you get a tuxedo in that?"

"Lots of practice."

"I'll believe it when I see it."

"Oh, you will." Preferably after a very steamy shower and skills with an iron that would make any mother proud.

"We have to get through customs first."

Gabe was scoping out the rest of the terminal, while Nathan eyed the snaking lines at the four customs stations. He was desperate for a hot meal and a hot shower, not necessarily in that order, but it looked like they'd be spending at least an hour or more in line.

It was more than an hour by the time their turn came. Closer to two. Much to Nathan's surprise, Gabe was relatively calm for the duration. Not that he was complaining.

The inspector seemed suspicious that the two of them only had one bag apiece, which was unusual, judging by the Brazilians coming through with enough luggage to put a Hollywood starlet to shame. The man's scowl got deeper when he saw how Nathan had all his clothing tightly bundle wrapped, folded over and around itself to make a neat package. Much to his relief, the inspector merely flipped back a few of the layers instead of pulling the whole thing apart, poked his fingers in the corners and checked all the pockets before shoving the bag back toward him. Nathan snapped the lid shut and zipped it. When he pulled it off the table, Gabe was already there waiting, his own bag in hand. "Pretty impressive."

"You thought I was lying?"

"Exaggerating maybe. Though I might have to ask you for pointers later."

It was then that Nathan noticed the slight crinkle of amusement around Gabe's smoky eyes. "Oh, my God, you actually have a sense of humor? Do you feel all right?"

"Shut up. The car should be this way." But there was no mistaking the smile as he turned and walked off.

He was a different man on the ground. The tie was gone, and his jacket was slung over his carry-on. Even as he flagged down the driver holding the placard with *N. Graves* on it, Nathan could tell his attention was still on the terminal at large and Nathan in particular. It was an unusual kind of attention, and Nathan thought he could get used to it.

"The secure car is waiting at the hotel," Gabe explained, handing Nathan's bag to the driver. "It made more sense to have one of my local contacts take us to the hotel and worry about orienting ourselves from there."

"I'll leave that to you. Navigating around a new city isn't my strong suit."

"Can't get by without GPS?"

"Until I know the territory, I prefer to let someone else lead the way."

Gabe gave him a wicked look and seemed about to say something, but instead opened the door for him and turned to instruct the driver.

Nathan really wished Gabe had said it. He suspected it would have been sharp and just a little bit dirty.

Conversation stayed at a minimum, save between Gabe and the driver, as the car sped through the streets of Rio toward their hotel. By the time they checked in and headed up to their rooms, Nathan had no attention for anything outside that hot shower and a very long nap. Good thing his meeting with local leaders wasn't until tomorrow evening. Plenty of time to rest up and get acclimated.

Gabe took Nathan's keycard and opened the door.

"I'm a big boy, Gabe. I can open my own door."

"Not when you've hired a bodyguard. Get used to it, Nathan." He went in the room first, checking the bathroom and the wardrobe as well as under the bed before allowing Nathan in.

Irritated, Nathan dropped his bag on the luggage rack, while Gabe closed the door behind him. "This isn't a James Bond movie."

"I could tell. If it was, there'd be a girl in your bed."

Startled, he stared at Gabe a minute before laughing out loud. "Wouldn't that be a thing?"

Gabe grinned as well before opening the joining door. "I'll be next door. Don't go out without me, and don't bring anyone here without letting me know."

"If I can't go out without you, how would I get anyone up here without you knowing? You think I'm going to call for a hooker?"

"If that's what you want to do, that's fine. You just have to let me know."

"It's not what I want to do."

"Might be better for both of us if it was."

Before Nathan could comment, Gabe slipped out and went to settle into his own room.

Nathan couldn't help smiling. Instead of growing more adamant that nothing was going to happen between them, Gabe seemed to be relenting. By very gradual degrees. Persistence could pay off.

But right now, shower.

Gabe apparently showered faster than he did because he was waiting in one of the club chairs in his room, more casually dressed and looking over the hotel menu, when Nathan knocked. A bit unnervingly, he had a holster strapped across his chest, and Nathan could just see the grip of an automatic tucked between his arm and ribs. "Room service or restaurant?"

"Out. Anywhere out. I won't last long, but I need some fresh air before I collapse for the night."

"Sounds good to me." Gabe dropped the menu on the table and stood up, reaching for the linen jacket hanging on the back of the desk chair.

"Where'd the gun come from? You couldn't have brought it on the flight."

"My local contact arranged for it when he set up the car. It was waiting for me."

"Convenient."

"Practical."

Scary was more apt. "Are you in the mood for anything in particular?"

"Something local."

"We'll ask the concierge on the way out."

The concierge directed them to a pleasant bistro about a five-minute walk from the hotel.

It was on the beach, but not one of the tourist hangouts, more of a place for the well-heeled locals to enjoy the ocean while avoiding the worst of the *turistas.*

Hand curled around his beer, Nathan closed his eyes and inhaled warm ocean air. "Oh yes, this is better."

"So much for the idealist." Gabe was smiling, taking the edge off his teasing. "You just wanted an excuse to go somewhere warm."

"It's not my fault some of the areas with the biggest problems are in decent climates. I suppose there's always Eastern Europe."

"No beaches in Afghanistan. You might want to rethink that."

There were a number of reasons Afghanistan hadn't been first on his list, lack of beaches not among them. The top reason was that he thought it might be easier to deal with drug lords than corporate-backed guerillas. An independent and relatively small venture also didn't stand a snowball's chance in Afghanistan and Iraq, the big moneymakers. The Americas provided the prefect place to establish yourself and help the underprivileged so frequently overlooked.

Nathan took another sip of his beer. "I really wish I could have started this in the US. Unfortunately, it wasn't until after Katrina that I saw what could, what needed to be done. And, frankly, it's easier for me to try to help here or in Africa rather than back home."

"Less politics."

"Different politics. It's harder when the self-righteous pork barrellers are your own people." To change the topic, he nodded at Gabe's bottled water. "No drinking while on the job, I presume?"

"Definitely not on the first day. Otherwise, it depends on the job and what I have to do to keep a low profile."

Nathan grinned around the neck of his bottle. "Here I thought maybe you didn't trust yourself around me with a couple of beers in you."

"I think I'm the one who needs to be worried."

"That is what I'm paying you for, I suppose."

"What, to let you sexually harass me?"

"No, to watch my ass." Nathan winked and took a drink.

Gabe rolled his eyes. "You're incorrigible."

"Well, it helps that you haven't told me to go fuck myself yet."

"You ignore me when I do."

"Then stop being polite. I'm a big boy, Gabe. I can take rejection."

Gabe didn't say anything. He turned his bottle on the table a couple of times and then took a drink, all the time staring out to the sea.

Time for a drastic topic change. "So, are you a diehard Cubs fan, or do you support a real baseball team?"

"Who says I'm a baseball fan at all?"

"It's as good a place to start as anywhere else."

They were saved having to make further conversation by the arrival of their food, thick grilled pork steaks and a hearty local stew called *feijoada*—beans, pork and beef simmered to salty perfection and served with rice, greens and thick slices of fried bananas. They set to work on the food, leaving Gabe's sudden discomfort behind.

When he finished, Gabe pushed his plate aside. "I have to admit, the food is what I miss most about not traveling."

Nathan smirked. "That's what most people bitch about."

"If you always go to the chains, yeah. But the local stuff...you never know what you're going to find."

"Not into sports, are into food. Got it. I'll have to make sure you get a chance to try the *moqueca* before we go."

Gabe leaned back in his seat. "I need to walk some of that off or I'm never going to sleep tonight. You want me to take you back to the hotel first?"

"I'll come with you. A walk on the beach at night sounds perfect."

"A perfect way to get mugged." Nevertheless, he sounded pleased.

"That's what I have my bodyguard for."

"You have a point."

"What? No argument?" Nathan asked as he flagged down the waiter.

Gabe smiled. "I've decided to choose my battles."

"No battle. We're on the same side." Nathan looked at the bill, left an appropriate number of *reals* he'd gotten at the hotel to cover the cost, and stood up. "Ready?"

"As I'll ever be," Gabe replied and followed him out.

CHAPTER 5

Music drifted down the shoreline from an assortment of seaside nightspots, still lacking the revelry of what would come later in the evening. The beach itself wasn't completely abandoned. A few evening strollers like themselves walked at various points near and away from the gentle waves.

Gabe would have been content to walk along the promenade that edged the Copacabana Beach in a wave of black and white stones, well-lit and lined with vendors, but Nathan insisted on ditching his shoes and rolling up his trousers to go down to the water's edge. There was no way Gabe could let him go alone. The Copacabana had a reputation at night, and Nathan had hired Gabe to do a job. So his own shoes came off and his own hems were rolled up. He left the jacket on, though.

"Tell me you're not enjoying this at least a little."

Gabe glanced over at Nathan and deadpanned, "I'm not enjoying this even a little."

"Liar."

He couldn't help smiling. "Let's just say I'm not used to relaxing."

"Really. I couldn't tell."

Gabe shrugged. "I've been putting a business together for the last five years. And was in the FBI for ten years before that. Not a lot of time for fun."

"All work and no play…"

"Even before the Bureau, I wasn't big on relaxing. You can relax when you're dead."

Nathan snorted. "But you sure as hell won't be able to enjoy it."

"Which I guess is rather the point."

Closer to the water, it was darker, the low waves lapping at the sand, lights from the promenade far beyond them reaching down to glint off the water. It was late now, almost midnight, but the lights of the city masked the stars in the inky sky above, making the few that did show through all the more precious somehow.

"Don't you ever do anything on the spur of the moment?"

"Not anymore." All of the hook-ups after Marcus, after the divorce—the few that there were—had been very carefully planned out on his end. Maybe it took some of the joy out of it, but it beat being caught with his pants down again.

"I'm sorry."

Of all the responses he had expected, that wasn't one of them. "Why sorry?"

"I think you miss out on a lot by planning out every moment of your life. There's something liberating about thinking, 'I want an ice cream cone' and getting one, even if it's not in your plan. Or going on a trip somewhere ridiculous at the last minute without even booking a hotel room. Or kissing someone on the spur of the moment."

And that was how Gabe ended up with warm, soft lips and the barest hint of stubble pressed against his own.

What surprised him most was that he was the one to kiss Nathan.

Nathan certainly didn't seem to mind. After the initial surprise, he relaxed, opening his mouth to Gabe and cupping his fingers along Gabe's jaw to guide him. It was slow and exploratory as Gabe learned the fullness of Nathan's lips, the delicate nip of his teeth, the plush strength of his tongue until somehow they were pressed together chest and thigh, and Nathan was pulling away for breath.

"Not that I'm complaining, but I certainly wasn't expecting that." Nathan's voice had dropped a half octave and the man was every bit as hard as Gabe was.

When he'd acted without thinking, he'd been fine. But now that he could think, Gabe stepped back, putting needed distance between them. "Sorry, I really shouldn't have done that."

Nathan reclaimed the space separating them. "Yes, you really should have." This time Nathan initiated the contact, and Gabe didn't have the desire to resist.

Nathan's hands were busy, caressing Gabe's chest, dropping down to grip his ass, ascending again to get lost in his hair. Gabe couldn't help responding in kind. Nathan felt good under his hands, solid and warm, responsive to his caresses. When he slipped a hand under the hem of Nathan's shirt to rest on the bare skin at the base of his spine, Nathan sucked in a breath.

"If we stop this to go back to the hotel"—Nathan sucked kisses along the underside of Gabe's jaw as he spoke—"are you going to think better of it and change your mind?"

"Probably."

"Then we'll have to stay here."

His kisses became even more intrusive, demanding, *wanting,* and it was all Gabe could do not to give in. He caught Nathan's wrists and stepped back, fighting his own need. "We can't do this here. Even Rio's not that open-minded."

"Which means we won't be doing it at all." Nathan already sounded resigned.

Gabe wished that weren't the case. But long-practiced discipline and common sense were already sliding back into place. "It's late, and we've both had a long day."

Nathan shoved his hands in his pockets, as if to stop himself from reaching out again. "The world didn't come to an end because you did something spur of the moment."

Gabe bent and picked up both pairs of shoes, which had dropped in the sand. "Who knew?"

The walk back up the beach and to their hotel was silent. Neither oppressive nor uncomfortable, just silent for lack of anything more to say.

"Stay here," Gabe said when they reached Nathan's door. He ducked inside and did a quick sweep. Probably unnecessary, but better safe than sorry. "All clear."

Nathan stepped into Gabe's personal space, and Gabe caught his breath in anticipation of the assault to come.

Only it didn't.

"Gonna be a long night, Gabe," he said, teasing and serious at the same time. "You know where to find me if you change your mind."

"I'm not going to assault you in the middle of the night."

"It's not assault if I want it." He brushed his shoulder against Gabe's chest as he passed to go into the bathroom, shutting the door behind him. A moment later, the shower started.

It was going to be a very long night indeed. And a shower probably wasn't a bad idea. A long, extremely cold shower.

WATCH MY BACK

CHAPTER 6

They started the next day with site visits.

It was just as well they jumped right into work. Nathan suspected if he had to spend a whole day with nothing to do but think about Gabriel Callan, he *would* end up accosting the man. As it was, he had had to spend some quality time with himself in the shower in order to get a decent night's sleep. He hadn't dared do it in bed for fear Gabe would hear him. He'd managed to keep from shouting at the last minute, but only barely.

Now they sat side by side in the front of the reinforced Audi Q5 Gabe had set up for their use, winding their way up one of the few passable roads into the Morro da Babilônia and the site for Nathan's project. There they would meet with the police commanders now in charge of the neighborhood since the ouster of the Third Command drug lords. Also on hand would be representatives of the *de facto* local council that had taken over day-to-day management of the issues the police couldn't be bothered with, not to mention a large number of security. Even with the removal of the drug cartels, the *favela* was far from safe for its residents, let alone any outsiders who came in.

Nathan felt better knowing Gabe had his back.

The sun shone in a clear sky, and the wind was light and warm, yet it might well be raining in the *favela* for the oppressive dreariness hanging over the residences. When you lived in such rough, dire conditions, you clung to whatever person promised to make it better. Even if you knew those promises were false.

Gabe was shaking his head.

"What?"

"You don't realize until it's right in front of you."

Nathan turned to look back down the mountain and nodded. "Two of the richest, most famous beaches in the whole world right there"— he gestured to Ipanema and Copacabana, which flanked the hillside where they stood—"and looking down on it, the most crushing poverty."

"Why have they left it here like this?"

"They haven't left it. The *favelas* get purged periodically, but Rio has no public housing program, so the people they displace end up coming back. There's always a temptation to gentrify a place like this, but that just pushes the poor out to move into other *favelas* or to start new ones. And until basic services are available, there will always be the threat of a return of the drug lords."

"Which is where you come in."

"Our houses are too small and basic for the middle class to want to settle in, but for the people who live here, a roof that doesn't leak and a bathroom that's more than a bucket in the corner are practically a miracle. It takes care of the people who need taking care of most, and if they can help themselves, then they'll hopefully begin to stand up for themselves on other issues as well."

A small group of men in suits and two camera crews awaited their arrival.

"So much for keeping a low profile," Nathan muttered to himself. He'd been hoping to put off dealing with the press until the dinner that evening. No such luck.

He couldn't speak Portuguese, and Gabe's was only good enough to get by, but fortunately, someone had thought far enough ahead to arrange a professional translator for talking to the press. Nathan straightened his jacket and got out of the car, all smiles and offered handshakes as Gabe came up behind him, a solid, secure presence.

Once the pleasantries and sound bites were out of the way, the reporters and cameras retreated, leaving Nathan and the suits to conduct their business.

They spent the whole day walking up hills, climbing stairs, talking to people, scaling more hills and more stairs until Nathan thought his legs would give out from the unaccustomed stress. Gabe never complained. He never said a word. True to their agreement, he didn't look threatening. His light clothes didn't scream "bodyguard," and he'd avoided the blackout aviator sunglasses for something softer that revealed his eyes. He smiled at the kids and held doors—or in most places worn curtains, back for the ladies—but he never lost awareness of where Nathan was, to the point where Nathan suspected they could blindfold Gabe and spin him in circles and he'd still unerringly point to Nathan.

Nathan wasn't sure if that was comforting or frightening.

The sun hung low on the horizon by the time they finished, leaving barely enough time to get back to the hotel and change for the evening. Exhausting though it was, the day felt productive, the residents of the *favelas* open and receptive to the housing project.

Nathan barely waited for Gabe to clear the room before he followed him in, dropping down in the club chair and ignoring the spectacular view out his window. "Christ, that was a long day."

Gabe chuckled. "It's not over yet."

"Thanks for reminding me."

"Anytime." He stopped at the door. "I'll be back in a half-hour?"

"Yeah, that's fine." Nathan waved him off and didn't move for a full ten minutes after Gabe left.

That didn't stop Nathan's brain from going interesting places when he heard Gabe's shower start.

Water and soap gliding down the muscular curves and flat planes of Gabe's skin, winter pale save his face and neck taking on a faint golden brown from their day out in the sun.

Nathan envied that soap.

Of course, even if he could drag himself into Gabe's shower, nothing would come of it. He was too wiped out at the moment to properly take advantage of his bodyguard. Maybe after a shower of his own and a ten-minute nap…

He groaned and shoved himself up out of the chair.

Right now, he was going to be lucky if he made it through the shower without falling asleep.

*   *   *

Dinner that evening had coffee and plenty of it. The shower had revived Nathan long enough to get dressed and to the event in functioning condition. But after exchanging yet another round of pleasantries and trying to get his point across to the reporters through his translator, he was about done. Alcohol was not on his menu for the

129

evening.

"You going to make it?" Gabe asked once they were seated at their table.

Nathan inhaled deeply over his fresh cup of coffee. "So long as the coffee holds out, I just might."

"That's your fourth cup tonight. I'll be surprised if you sleep at all."

"I can think of other reasons to lose sleep that would be far more enjoyable, but I'll survive."

"Do you really think now's the best time to be flirting?"

"Hey, whatever keeps me awake."

Gabe shook his head. "You've got two more cups before I'm cutting you off."

Nathan knew he shouldn't mention the half a pot he'd had back at the hotel, then. "Yes, nanny."

"Hey, I'm pointing out that you haven't had much to eat today and you still have to pull off your presentation in front of a roomful of people with a spotty understanding of English. Rattling it off at ninety miles an hour because of a caffeine buzz probably won't help the situation."

"Neither will my falling asleep halfway through."

Gabe just held up two fingers.

Bastard.

The food arrived, saving him from caffeine poisoning.

Conference food in Brazil wasn't that much different than it was in the States, just with a different set of side dishes. Nathan didn't care at this point. The caffeine had dulled his sense of taste and his appetite, but Gabe was watching, so he ate everything in front of him. He hadn't realized when he hired a bodyguard that he was getting a mother as well. Considering his current attraction to the man, the thought was more than a little disturbing.

Thankfully, he was second on the evening's agenda of speakers. The slide show spoke for itself, so Nathan's commentary, run through a translator, was less pivotal than it would have been to an English speaking audience. Fewer jokes, not as many flourishes. Just as well. He was too tired to extemporize.

He finished to a flattering round of applause and returned to his seat. "I need to get through another hour and then I can leave without causing any offense," he informed Gabe. "Since you've cut off my supply, it's up to you to prevent an international incident."

The next speaker took the podium to talk about something related to the expansion of the Metro system and spoke entirely in Portuguese. Nathan was dead.

Until he felt Gabe's shoeless foot curl around his ankle.

His shock must have showed. "Good to see you're paying attention. But try not to give the game away, all right?" Gabe's smile was wickedness personified.

His foot was gone, but the sensation of it lingered, warming up Nathan's leg to tingle somewhere just south of his groin. It was tempting to close his eyes to see if Gabe would do it again, but now he was too alert, waiting for Gabe's next move. It was an evil, evil ploy, and it had worked.

The anticipation kept Nathan wide-awake until they were able to leave. And Gabe hadn't done a single thing after that first too-brief contact.

"That was cruel," Nathan said when they were finally on their way back to the hotel. "Making promises you aren't going to follow through on."

"I made no promises." Gabe looked smug in the dashboard lights, the LED glow emphasizing the faint dimples in his cheeks.

"You flirted with me."

"I touched you. Once. Innocently. You said prevent an international incident, so…"

"Cocktease."

Gabe snorted. "Oh, I haven't even begun."

"Okay, now that *was* a promise."

His grin got wider.

Nathan was quite certain the buzz he felt wasn't from the caffeine anymore. "Drive faster."

"No. I like to avoid speeding tickets in foreign countries. And in general."

He stroked his hand roughly over Gabe's thigh, making him hiss in surprise. "How do you feel about handjobs on foreign highways?"

He thought he was going to get shot down again when Gabe looked at him. "Don't like them as much as blowjobs."

"God damn it! Are you trying to make me crazy?"

"Turnabout's fair play." Gabe winked at him. *Winked* at him.

If Gabe was bluffing, Nathan was damn well going to call it. He dragged his hand farther up Gabe's thigh, across his very evident arousal to the top of his trousers.

Gabe didn't take his eyes off the road, but one eyebrow went up expectantly.

Nathan unfastened Gabe's belt, popped the button, and inched the zipper down. Gabe kept driving.

"All that denial talk was just to get my attention, wasn't it?"

"Not at all. Maybe you've managed to overcome my better judgment at last."

"Thank God. I was worried it was going to take the whole time here to wear you down."

"So what are you waiting for?"

Good question.

He fit his hand in through the front of Gabe's fly, relishing the hard ridge of Gabe's cock against his palm. Even the fabric of Gabe's briefs couldn't hide the heat of it from Nathan's touch. It was enough to make his mouth water, appropriately enough.

"We're here."

"What?"

Gabe pulled into the drive in the front of their hotel. "We're here."

Nathan pulled his hand out. "You did that on purpose."

Gabe grinned, zipped up his pants, and got out of the car.

Damn it. Nathan was going to make him pay. Somehow. After he fucked him senseless.

He restrained himself as they crossed the lobby, but as soon as the elevator doors closed, he shoved Gabe against the wall, assaulting his mouth at the same time he returned his hand to its earlier exploration.

Gabe didn't hold back this time, hands in Nathan's hair as he took control of the kiss, shoving back at Nathan so he was the one against the wall. Christ, he wanted this so damn badly.

All too soon the elevator reached their floor. Gabe hastily did up his pants and exited first, still on the job. This starting and stopping was getting old fast.

After doing his now-familiar check of Nathan's room, Gabe hauled Nathan in and shoved him up against the closing door. "Now, where were we?"

Nathan didn't bother answering, hauling Gabe in for another kiss and maneuvering him back toward the bed.

Gabe refused to be bested and twisted at the last minute, dropping Nathan onto the soft mattress first, following him down to trap him there, his mouth now making forays along Nathan's jaw to his ear and neck.

Nathan scrabbled at Gabe's pants, determined get them open for good and off before Gabe could change his mind.

Gabe, though, seemed to be in no hurry. He caught Nathan's hands and drew them up over his head, pinning them there while he took his time tasting all the skin between Nathan's earlobe and the open collar of his shirt.

It felt so good, and Nathan gave himself up to it, the warmth, the safety, the promise of satisfaction soaking through him, relaxing him, making the world fade away.

By the time he realized he was falling asleep, it was already too late.

CHAPTER 7

It was Nathan's near unresponsiveness that alerted Gabe to the fact something was going on. The gentle snore drove the point home.

He really should have cut Nathan's coffee off sooner.

Chuckling, he pulled away. Nathan was in a frenzy for this to happen, but Gabe didn't mind taking time and letting it unfold naturally. Although he had been looking forward to undressing him.

Of course, he still had the chance.

Clinically rather than erotically, he slipped off Nathan's shoes and worked the tuxedo jacket off him. He debated for a moment before undoing his belt and taking off his pants, leaving him in black boxer briefs. He took off the tie, but left the shirt and rolled him under the turned back bed linens. "Sleep tight, Romeo."

Nathan didn't stir once.

Slipping out, Gabe went to his own room. It was going to be another night of fitful sleep.

He was just undressing when his phone vibrated. *Jeannie.*

"What's wrong?" he answered.

"Well, hello to you, too, Gabriel."

"Jeannie, you're calling me in the middle of the night. So I ask again, what's wrong?"

"We've got a mole."

"A mole?"

"Planted by your good buddy Deguerre."

"What the hell is he doing? How did you find out?"

"Did Nathan tell you he talked to Deguerre back in Baltimore the same day he'd seen you?"

Gabe clenched his teeth. "No, he didn't."

"Relax, hero, he shot him dead. I've been talking to Nathan's assistant. Cute kid. Deguerre knew all the details about the contract with us and tried to convince Nathan to throw us over for him."

"I suppose Nathan wanting my ass worked in our favor," Gabe said bitterly.

"Yes, darling, this whole deal hinged on whether or not you'd put out," Jeannie deadpanned. "Which, judging by your current attitude, you haven't."

"No, the attitude is because Deguerre's trying to fuck me over. Again."

"And because you aren't getting any."

"I would've if Nathan hadn't fallen asleep!" Only after the words left his mouth did he realized he'd played right into Jeannie's hands. *Again.*

"Damn, you must really be out of practice if that happened."

"Jeannie, we've got bigger problems than my sex life right now."

"Lack of, you mean."

"Jeannie."

"Yes, yes. I found the culprit. It's one of the new local security guys we hired when we put Kyle and Stillwater on international duty. The guy's got bigger aspirations than stadium show duty, and Deguerre promised it to him."

"How'd you find out?"

"He was a jackass to Hettie, flashing a lot of extra cash. It was an easy research job to track the money back to Dagger. So what do you want me to do?"

There really wasn't much they could do, aside from remaining alert and keeping an eye out for anything else Deguerre might try. "Watch and listen."

"All right. I've already got his phone records, and we put a bug on his phone this afternoon."

"You know that's not admissible."

"No, but it'll give us a heads-up if he tries anything. And I'm putting him to work in the office. Maybe he'll give us enough rope to hang him and Deguerre, too."

Hanging Deguerre was far too appealing. "I appreciate the warning, Jeannie."

"Hold on. You're not hanging up on me yet," she cut him off. "What's going on with you and Nathan?"

"Good night, Jeannie."

"Gabe—" He could hear the amusement in her voice as he hung up.

His own brief flare of good humor quickly dissipated. Now he was going to have to pull double duty. It wasn't just pissed off drug lords and other supporters of the status quo he had to look out for, but now he also had to be alert to anything Deguerre would do to screw him over.

Once upon a time, in their early days at the Bureau, they'd been...well, not friends, but less antagonistic to one another. But then there had been service commendations and Jeannie and a very clear difference of opinion on what their jobs were. Gabe was an agent to serve his country and just maybe get the hell out of Hopkinton, Iowa, and have a bit of adventure. Deguerre was an agent solely as a means to an end. Make connections, gain power and influence to gain more power and more influence.

When he'd gone too far and Gabe had called him on it, he'd taken it personally. By the time Gabe had gotten sick of the politics and retired, the resentment had grown into a full-blown grudge that Deguerre had taken with him into the private sector.

Gabe rubbed his eyes tiredly. *Screw Deguerre.* He was tired, and they had another long day tomorrow tromping up and down through the narrow walkways and shanties of the *favelas*. Right now, he just wanted to sleep. He needed to sleep. He had a job to do first and foremost; the trouble with Deguerre and Gabe's growing attraction to Nathan were both secondary to his role as bodyguard. It had to be.

Maybe after this assignment was done...

CHAPTER 8

He woke to the feel of a warm tongue licking over his stomach.

"God, you're a heavy sleeper." Nathan sucked a kiss just below Gabe's navel before grinning up at him. "Anyone could have broken in here, and you wouldn't have heard a thing."

Gabe caught a handful of Nathan's hair and tugged him up until they were face to face. "What are you doing in my bed?"

Unrepentant, Nathan sucked on Gabe's bottom lip. "We were interrupted last night."

"You fell asleep."

"If you hadn't drawn things out for so long, I would have been wide awake and a full participant."

"Because the six cups of coffee—"

"And the half pot I had before we left the hotel."

Gabe felt his eyes go wide of their own volition. "The caffeine content is higher down here. You're lucky you didn't collapse from sheer toxicity."

Nathan placed a kiss at the end of his chin. "I'm really going to have to re-read that contract. I don't remember there being a mother clause."

"There isn't a sex clause, either. That mean this isn't going to happen?"

"Wouldn't that be to prohibit, not encourage it?" Nathan ran his tongue along the edge of Gabe's jaw, pulling lightly at the stubble and making Gabe shiver at the sensation.

"Depends on the contract, doesn't it?" He relaxed his grip to comb his fingers through Nathan's coarse hair and then down over his back. He'd ditched the shirt somewhere between his bed and Gabe's. *Christ.* "And how the hell did you get in here?"

Nathan nodded toward the wall. "Used the adjoining door."

Which had been securely locked on Gabe's side. He'd checked. "It's a deadbolt."

"You don't have to be an ex-agent to know how to get a locked door open."

"Wouldn't it have been easier to go to the front desk and make up some plausible excuse?"

Nathan grinned. "Tried that. But they seem to pride themselves on their security measures here."

"Except when it comes to doors to adjoining rooms."

Nathan slithered his body along Gabe's. "If you really want me to leave—"

Gabe rolled them and had Nathan pinned beneath him before he could finish the sentence.

"I'll take that as a no, then."

In response, Gabe took possession of Nathan's mouth with a fierce, claiming kiss, leaving them both in no doubt about where things were heading between them.

Gabe had known all along, regardless of his protests. Nathan was too attractive a package to let pass. His intelligence and dry wit, coupled with a compassion that drove him to action, were all qualities Gabe found every bit as appealing as Nathan's lithe body and dark eyes. It had never been a question of if, but when.

The answer seemed to be now.

He shoved Nathan's soft sleep pants down his legs, then dropped back to press naked skin to naked skin.

Nathan chuckled. "Do you always sleep in the nude, or just when you're hoping to get lucky?"

"I used to be married. I always got lucky when I was sleeping."

Nathan's grin got bigger. "No wonder Jeannie left you."

"At least she never fell asleep on me."

"Oh, low blow." Nathan drifted his hand lower. "Speaking of low blows…"

Gabe rolled them over again so Nathan was on top. "Show me what you've got."

"I'm wide awake, no caffeine."

"Yeah, but once burned and all that, so I prefer to hedge my bets."

Nathan captured Gabe's mouth again, this time slow and sensual, tasting rather than attacking. His body undulated against Gabe's as Gabe twisted his fingers in Nathan's hair, holding him in place. The sensuality of it went beyond last night's rut and made Gabe at least partly glad Nathan had fallen asleep. He much preferred it like this.

He had to be a realist, though. "We have to be back out in the *favela* by nine."

Nathan licked a shuddering line along Gabe's jaw. "Plenty of time."

"Not for all I have in mind."

Blunt teeth nipped at his ear. "Well, we'll just have to save something for later then."

It was tempting to take the top again. "We've only got two weeks."

"Optimist."

Nathan began working his way day, almost serpentine in his movement and never once breaking contact.

Gabe hated it at the same time he reveled in it. He wanted to be the one touching Nathan, driving Nathan crazy.

Well, why didn't he?

With a gentle shove, he pushed Nathan onto the mattress and turned himself around so they were end to end, each free to taste each other, torment each other at the same time.

"God, you really have no fear, do you?"

"Fear keeps you from getting things done." Hauling Nathan close, Gabe licked a long stripe along the underside of his cock. While Nathan had been responsive last night, fully alert and decaffeinated was even better.

Nathan got even by tonguing one of Gabe's balls into his mouth with a soft suck.

"God!"

Nathan chuckled and released him. "You are going to be so easy."

In retaliation, Gabe swallowed him whole.

"Oh, Jesus, Gabe!"

Gabe sucked off the tip with a wet pop. "Now who's easy?"

They soon got lost in an escalation of pleasure and obscenities, until Nathan put a restraining hand on Gabe's forehead. "Not like this. I want to you to fuck me."

Gabe would be a fool to turn down an offer like that.

He rolled off, but was surprised to find Nathan already holding up a condom. "I didn't come in here just to get held up if you weren't enough of a Boy Scout."

Gabe snatched it out of his hand. "And here I thought you were a romantic."

Nathan rose to his knees and pulled Gabe down to kiss him, hand drifting down his arm. To Gabe's surprise, Nathan took the condom from him. He put it in his mouth with a waggle of his eyebrows and bent down to slide mouth and rubber around Gabe's cock. He worked it so carefully down with his tongue that, by the time he was done, Gabe just about was as well.

Pulling back, Nathan reclined on the bed, eyes dancing with devilish amusement. "How's that for romantic?" He held out a tube of lubricant to Gabe.

"Turnabout's fair play," was all Gabe said as he moved between Nathan's outstretched thighs, easing his legs up and exposing him completely.

Fair didn't really enter into it. Gabe took his time, first teasing his slicked index finger around the tight pucker. He sucked along Nathan's neck, feeling every gasp and groan against his lips as he worked one finger in, then two. Nathan wrapped a leg around him in encouragement, as though his reactions weren't encouragement enough.

At three fingers, Nathan writhed beneath him, begging until Gabe finally replaced his fingers with his cock. Gabe was only human after all. And he soon found that the little control he'd regained quickly dissipated the farther he plunged into Nathan's body.

Nathan propped himself up on one elbow, watching as Gabe buried his cock in him again and again, his head rolling, his hips arching, moaning, threatening, but never looking away for long. Gabe decided to make it easier for him, rising up on his knees and catching Nathan's legs in the crook of his arms, opening him up to slam into him in long, deep strokes that had both of them cursing.

He batted Nathan's hand out of the way as he reached for his cock, fisting him in a near brutal rhythm.

Nathan only encouraged him, demanding more, meeting every thrust to drive him deeper, never quiet, never still, noisy and messy and the best sex Gabe could remember ever having.

With that thought, he came, driving one last time into Nathan's clenching heat. Nathan's hand covered Gabe's, bringing himself off with a few quick strokes.

Breathless, sweaty, and more content than he could recall, Gabe lay atop Nathan and savored the moment.

Nathan held him closer, tangling legs and arms around him, burying his face in the hollow of Gabe's neck with a satisfied chuckle. "Now, that was worth waiting for."

Gabe huffed out a laugh of his own. "You think it wouldn't have been as good last night?"

"Oh, it would have been good, but it'll make tonight even better." He ground against Gabe seductively. "We haven't had time to get used to it yet. So every time I look over at you and find you watching me, every time you brush up against me, we're both going to be so worked that by the time we get back here, we'll be desperate to rip each other's clothes off and screw ourselves stupid all night."

Gabe rolled his hips. "I'm ready to do that now."

Nathan kissed him quickly. "We have to be up in Babilonia in an hour." He slipped out from under Gabe and grabbed his hand. "Come on. You need a shower."

Gabe let him draw him to his feet, not stopping until he was pressed against Nathan again. "Can I wash your back?"

Nathan ran a hand up Gabe's arm and down his chest. "You can wash whatever you like, as long as we get to the site on time."

They made it with two minutes to spare.

CHAPTER 9

"Why didn't you tell me about Deguerre approaching you?"

Nathan looked up from the foundation he was inspecting. They were alone for the moment. "It didn't seem important. Unless my guy turned up anything outside it being a standard client-poaching attempt."

"Nothing's standard where Deguerre's involved."

"How did you find out?"

"Your assistant called Jeannie. Turned out Deguerre had a mole in our organization." Gabe seemed to take it as a personal affront, and Nathan could not really blame him. "You should have told me. It's my job to look out for those types of things."

He shrugged. "It didn't seem that important."

Gabe eyed him sharply. "Not important, yet you still had your assistant check him out."

Nathan folded his arms over his chest. "I don't like it when other people try to tell me how to do my business."

"I'm responsible for your safety. Deguerre falls under that."

"Or you're just pissed because you're the last to know. I must have missed the clause on full disclosure."

Gabe rubbed his eyes, a gesture Nathan found irresistibly vulnerable. "It's not like that. Deguerre likes to get in my way. Down here, I can't do anything to stop him. If I'd known—"

"You wouldn't have come down?"

Gabe looked pained.

"Then I don't regret the choice for a minute." Nathan dared to stroke Gabe's arm, enjoying the skitter of electricity coiling low in his belly at the contact. "I want you here. Deguerre can fuck himself."

"You should be careful what you say, *senhor*. These walls have ears."

Nathan half expected to find them surrounded by several well-armed men. Instead, a lone, weathered man leaned against the whitewashed shed behind them, idly smoking a rolled cigarette.

Gabe straightened, and Nathan could almost see the gun that would leap into his hand if this turned into a threat. "Most of these walls don't understand English."

"Most. Not all. Not all the ears here are *favelados*." The man glanced over their shoulders at the police and officials discussing local politics in rapid Portuguese. "Come with me."

Nathan could almost see Gabe calculating various scenarios and outcomes, potential dangers... "Stay very close," Gabe finally told Nathan. "Lead on, *senhor*."

The man took one last glance behind them, dropped his cigarette and ground it out with a toe, then turned with his hands in his pockets and sauntered into the maze of shacks without another word. Nathan wasn't sure which way was up, let alone where they were, by the time the man stopped in front of a slightly less dilapidated structure. "Please, come in."

Nathan looked to Gabe for confirmation, receiving a tight nod in return. Gabe remained near the door when he followed them in.

"You are in danger here." The man's slouching, casual demeanor disappeared in the privacy of the shack. He was straighter now, more aware and more than a little anxious. "The drug lords, they've been quiet and left us alone since the government ran them out. Perhaps they were biding their time. But now they've heard about the plans you bring to rebuild the *favelas* for the *moradores da favela,* and they are afraid. They know if that happens, if the people are independent, they will never reclaim Babilonia and will lose the others one by one as they are converted. They are coming here, now, to take Babilonia back."

"Wait...now as in today?" And the day had started so well.

"*Si,* that is the plan."

"And why are you telling us this?" Gabe asked darkly.

"Because I am in favor of what *Senhor* Graves is trying to do. It is time the people took control of their own lives."

Gabe grabbed Nathan's arm and shoved him toward the door. "We're getting back to the hotel. Now."

They had barely set foot on the narrow path when an explosion shattered the air, deafening them as a black cloud rose up past the edge of the roof line. A rattle of gunfire followed the echoing thunder.

"No." The man stepped in front of Gabe, brooking no argument. "It is too late. That was your vehicle. They will be looking for you now. They will be watching the retreats from this place and will have their spies looking. You must hide."

The idea clearly didn't sit well with Gabe. It sure didn't with Nathan.

"But we must hurry."

"Do we really have a choice?" Nathan ventured.

"Damn it, no, we don't." Gabe growled. "I will shoot you if you betray us," he told their companion.

"Of that, I have no doubt. Come." The hunched over posture was back as the man led them deeper into the *favela* maze.

They could hear fighting in the distance, but getting closer, even as they tried to get farther away. The streets, barely wide enough for them to walk two astride, were empty, balls left where they'd fallen, shutters down on the ramshackle windows.

"They know what's coming," their guide said, noticing Nathan's gaze.

"What's coming?"

The man paused to look behind them, then gestured them to a steep, rickety stairway going down. "The cartels will fight with the police through the night, but by morning they will control the *favela*. Tomorrow will be quiet as they sort the loyal and the traitors from those who don't care so long as they are fed. Then the military will come, and it will begin again."

"Christ."

Gabe seemed as alert as their guide, and just as tense. "What's your name, friend?" he asked.

Nathan was surprised he hadn't thought to ask that himself.

"Cibran." He was still searching the streets, even as he shook Gabe's hand. "It won't matter soon. I'm taking you to the care of another."

"It matters to me. Thank you."

"Change matters to me. So I suppose we are even," Cibran said as he led them up to a blue clapboard structure butted against the hillside. He gave three short raps and the door opened. A woman poked her head out, eyes as dark as her hair and glaring at Cibran.

"*Eu sou pesaroso,* Alda."

The first was an apology to Alda, but everything else Cibran said after was gibberish to Nathan's untrained ear.

Her posture didn't relax any, but she did step back, opening the door farther, when Cibran had finished.

"In."

Gabe went first, not surprisingly, eyes scanning the small, dark room before gesturing Nathan in. There was nothing to the room—a battered table and chair, a bucket, a battered coffee can that seemed to serve as a makeshift stove. Daylight leaked in around the corrugated steel covering the windows, the only illumination in the room.

Cibran shoved past them and into a back room. Alda shooed them after him.

Already he had moved a worn cast iron bed aside and pulled up a piece of old carpet to reveal a hole. "In. You will hide here until tonight. I will send someone for you. Do you have an American coin? Something small, unimportant."

They both fished around in their pockets until Nathan came up with a quarter, one of the state quarters with a picture of Missouri on one side. Cibran snatched it out of his hand. "You will know it is them when they give you this back. Now go." He shoved a small knapsack into Gabe's hands and pushed them toward the hole.

Down they went and soon the floor dropped back over them, followed by the carpet, then bed. This was not how the day was supposed to end up.

Nathan heard a jangle of keys, and suddenly there was a bright spotlight in Gabe's hand. "Sorry, should've warned you."

"Don't be. I'm just glad we aren't stuck here in the dark for six to ten hours."

It wasn't much more than a hole they were in. The walls were chiseled, tool marks easily visible even in the narrow beam of light from Gabe's flashlight. The space was barely four feet square, just enough room for the two of them to sit on the floor rather than stand. Not that they could have stood, even if they'd wanted to. They both had to hunch over as it was.

There was a small battery-powered lamp on the wall. Nathan turned it on. "Better save your batteries in case we need them later."

Nodding, Gabe settled himself on the floor and started going through the bag. A couple bottles of water apiece, some dried food, a flashlight, spare batteries, and a random assortment of *centavo* coins totaling a little more than a couple of *reals*. This certainly didn't seem to be the first time Cibran had done this.

Gabe held up a deck of cards. "Entertainment. Cibran thought of everything."

Nathan was already feeling the walls close around him. "Yeah, convenient."

"What's wrong?"

"Don't you think it's a little weird he was there just in time to 'rescue' us?"

"I've seen stranger things."

That irritated Nathan. "How can you be so okay with this? They could just be keeping us here for the drug lords to come claim us."

"It's a possibility. However, it's an acceptable risk."

"Acceptable!"

Gabe put a firm hand on his shoulder. "Keep it down. And, yes, acceptable. Maybe this is a trap, maybe not. In either case, we're still safer in this hole than trying to make our way down the mountain with the worst of the fighting going on."

"Gabe—"

"Relax." He was soothing, not condescending, which Nathan appreciated. "If we were prisoners, they'd have left a better guard than one little old lady. If it starts to look dicey, we'll get out of here, but for right now, our best bet is to just sit tight. Didn't your mother ever teach you that in case you got lost as a kid?"

"She might've, if she'd ever let me out of her sight." Nathan grimaced. "This may be cruel to say, but if she hadn't died when I was eleven, I would have been a much different person."

"Are you sure your name's not really Norman?"

Nathan gave him a puzzled look.

"A boy's best friend is his mother? From *Psycho*?"

"Okay, I can't have gone stir crazy already. We've only been in here five minutes."

Gabe grinned and started shuffling the cards. "Just wait. By hour two, you'll be ready to kill me just for something to do."

"Oh, I can think of plenty for us to do…"

"Nathan."

"Can't blame a guy for trying." He sighed. "So what are we playing?"

"Hearts or gin rummy?"

"Not poker?"

"I suck at poker. I'd like to play something I have a shot at winning."

Nathan chuckled. "I'll keep that in mind. Let's go for gin."

CHAPTER 10

Gabe kept it calm, almost playful, for Nathan's sake, but inside he could feel his guts knotting. Even through the stone, or more likely through the thin boards covering their hideout, he could hear the bark of AK-47s and Uzis spitting death at one another. As they started drifting nearer, he tensed, the truth of their situation exquisitely clear to him.

No matter what, he had to keep Nathan safe.

He'd learned a long time ago in situations like this not to look at his watch. That was a good way to make yourself crazy. But when he heard voices upstairs, brusque male voices and one creaking, determined one, he did a quick time check. Three hours. Not soon enough to be their next escort, then.

"What—" Nathan started, but Gabe slapped a hand over his mouth, watching the ceiling as if he could see through wood.

There was a lot of stomping and a fair amount of shouting, mostly from Alda. The little he could make out from the smattering of Portuguese he knew, Alda was quite fed up the men barging into homes just because they had big guns and little dicks. Their mothers would weep if they saw their sons treat an old woman so roughly.

Gabe was torn between admiration and wishing Alda would play nice, though the tongue lashing seemed to do the trick, since soon the brutes were backing out.

He felt a tap on his arm and only then realized he still had Nathan in a near chokehold. "Sorry." He breathed the word against Nathan's ear as he released him.

"In another situation, I might consider that foreplay." Nathan's voice was rough with fear and equally quiet.

Gabe didn't take his eyes off the ceiling. "In another situation, it might be."

"I hope we get to test that out."

They crouched there, waiting for several tense minutes for whatever was coming next. All that came was the sound of the firefight growing more distance and an uneasy stillness settling into the house above them.

They both jumped when a bony hand thrust under the rug and dropped bananas and several purple, wrinkled fruits on their heads.

Gabe relaxed. "All clear." He handed Nathan one of the bananas and picked up one of the purple fruits to inhale its fragrance. "Passion fruit." He took out his Leatherman and started cutting it open.

Nathan found a dirty, folded piece of paper among the fruit.

He handed the note to Gabe, who smiled as he read it.

Cibran say 7 be ready go. Son of cartel. Dead. No love. Senhors *safe with Alda.*

"I think you have at least two supporters here."

"Amazing what people will do if they think someone gives a damn about them. What time is it now?"

"Only three."

"Jesus." Nathan rubbed his face.

"It could be worse."

"Oh?"

"It could only be two."

Nathan snorted in response. "Mr. Optimistic. I would've pegged you more for the cynical type."

Gabe popped a piece of fruit into his mouth, savoring the rich, sweet flavor. "Can't be cynical in this line of work. Practical, yes. Realistic, definitely. But if you're always believing and expecting the worst, you might as well give up at the start and make it easier for everyone involved."

Nathan reached over for a piece of the passion fruit, popped it in his mouth and chewed experimentally. He must have decided it was good because he took another one and handed Gabe a banana. Nothing Freudian there. "At least the food's not bad."

"At least there's food."

"True." Nathan grew quiet. "So going with a case of when and not if…*when* we get out of this *favela,* are we safe going back to the hotel? Or do we need to high-tail it to the embassy and get the hell out of Dodge?"

"I'm not sure." Gabe cut off another hunk of passion fruit, dumping the seeds in the corner. "Usually, the fighting in these skirmishes stays contained in the individual neighborhoods, and the hotel is far enough away that if we can get clear, we should be fine. Right now, I'm more worried about getting clear."

"Getting clear." There was the faintest hint of panic in Gabe's words.

Panic wouldn't do either of them any good. "Tell me about where you grew up."

"What?"

"Your hometown. Where you went to school. That sort of thing."

"Now's really not—"

"Now's the perfect time. We've got four hours to kill. Might as well get to know each other."

Gabe rubbed his leg against Nathan's as he encouraged him to talk, trying to keep him grounded physically while keeping his mind busy. Gabe had trained for these situations, had spent more than his share of time on surveillance in a crappy apartment or hiding in dark basements or even once, God help him, in a sewer for six hours. Nathan, though, was a social creature, used to being around people, always having someone to bounce ideas off. For now, Gabe was going to have to be that person.

He didn't really mind.

The more Nathan talked, the easier the words seemed to come to him, and the more at ease he became.

"And then my dad took me fly-fishing. Complete disaster."

Movement sounded above them, cutting off conversation. Quarter to seven. Early could be good or bad.

Soon the floorboards drew back and a lean youth, no older than his early teens, poked his head down. "You two going to keep talking all night or do you want to do some running?" He flipped a piece of silver down to them. It was Nathan's quarter from earlier. "The old man sends his apologies for not being able to come himself."

Gabe patted Nathan on the shoulder and boosted himself out of the hole, then reached down to help Nathan out as well. "Who are you?"

"Davi. Cibran's friends with my *papi.*"

"Your English is pretty good there, Davi."

"Comes from tricking all the tourists down at the beach. You pick up a lot when they think you're an ignorant *favelado*. Now come on."

"Where are we going?" Gabe was following regardless, guiding Nathan ahead of him.

"Safest place in the world. Territory the Baroes da Montanha have already searched."

"Occupied territory?"

"The closer you are to danger, the farther you are from harm."

Nathan didn't look impressed. "Oh, great. Just what we needed—a Brazilian hobbit."

"They were always underestimating the hobbits, no? A good thing to be, I think." Davi narrowed his eyes. "Though if you're calling me short, we may be having words."

"Give me a break, kid. What are you, twelve?"

Davi grinned. "Six. I'm tall for my age. Come on. We don't have much time."

As they were leaving, Gabe turned to Alda. "*Obrigado. Sua ajuda foi apreciada muito.*"

She gave him a toothy smile and shoved him out the door.

If navigating the *favelas* in the daylight was confusing, nighttime was far worse.

Davi didn't rely on lights as they crept up the steeply sloped walks, down ancient, swaying staircases, over battered tin roofs, until even Gabe was turned around. Their only reference points were the beaches—sometimes Copacabana, sometimes Ipanema—far below them and the ruddy glow of building fires much, much closer.

"If those get out of control," Nathan murmured, horrified, "they could take out the whole neighborhood."

"The *baroes* don't care." Davi didn't look back, still guiding them. "Now they're back, they want revenge."

Davi explained how the cartels maintained power through fear, and there was no greater fear than destroying what little the *favelados* possessed.

Down from the roofs, they crept again through the silent neighborhood. Here there were signs of fighting earlier, shanties marked with red spray paint, stains on the road that weren't water.

"Are you sure about this?"

Davi nodded. "Cibran says you stay inside, keep quiet, no one will bother you. Almost there."

He darted around a corner and froze.

Pacing through the intersection not twenty feet away was a soldier. He wore a nondescript black uniform and carried a high-powered carbine, but Gabe couldn't tell if he was friend or foe. Davi obviously could, though, crouching down so the long stairs that came out at the junction hid them from the man's gaze.

Gabe was tired of hiding.

Getting Nathan's attention, he touched his lips, then did the same to Davi before pulling out his gun. He crept closer, mindful of the detritus in the narrow passage, until the only thing between him and the soldier was the rickety stairway. The man turned, and Gabe leaped forward, clubbing the soldier into unconsciousness and dragging the body back into the alley. Davi and Nathan joined him, quickly hiding the man under a pile of rubbish.

Gabe had bigger things to worry about.

"What in the hell—" He popped the magazine out of the carbine, found it fully loaded, put it back in and cocked it. "This is an M4A1."

"So?" Nathan didn't look impressed.

"It's American. Hell, half our boys in Afghanistan don't have these things yet. Drug dealers usually make do with whatever old weapons they can scrounge up, usually Russian Kalashnikovs or AKMs. So how the hell did they get top of the line military grade hardware down here?"

"Outside funding isn't unheard of," Nathan said dismissively. "Probably some enterprising businessman hoping to profit from the chaos."

"No, you don't understand. These are government contract. They've only been rolling them out since the end of '09. You can't get this outside of the US military."

"We don't have time, *senhors.*" Davi looked nervous now, glancing up and down the road. "Come on, up."

Gabe slung the carbine over his shoulder and followed them up the stairs they'd hidden behind.

The marked *favela* Davi ushered them into was an utter disaster inside. What little furniture and belongings the former resident had were strewn haphazardly around.

"They will have been looking for anything of value. Such as it is in this place."

Gabe kept a careful lookout from the shadows near the window. "How long do you think before we can make a break back to town?"

Davi shook his head. "Not yet. Not tonight. Wait for Cibran. He'll know."

Nathan righted a chair, but didn't sit down, just gripped the back of it. "So we just wait here?"

"You wait. Keep the shutters closed. Don't go out. Everything you need is here."

"I need a beer and a hot shower."

The playful kid who had met them at Alda's was gone. Now Davi looked tense. "You want those things, *senhor;* you don't need them. Spoiled Americans." He darted out the door, then stuck his head back in. "Keep this shut." He shoved the sheet metal door in place and vanished.

"I think I preferred the hole in the ground," Nathan groused, dropping into the chair he'd uprighted. He scrubbed his face. "Though Davi's right. Spoiled American. A little discomfort and all I can do is bitch. We're alive and in one piece. What else matters?"

Gabe straightened the table and laid the M4A1 on it. "A lot. Although at least now we have windows to jump out of if we get cornered. I'm going to go look for a back door."

"I'm not going anywhere."

By the time Gabe returned from his quick inspection, he found Nathan with his head on his arms, snoring gently.

It was tempting to let him sleep, but neither of them needed him with a crick in his neck or worse when he woke up. Gabe nudged him gently. "Bed's in the back. Go lay down."

Nathan didn't protest, just stood up and shambled through the door. A moment later, Gabe heard the bedsprings creak. He pulled out the deck of cards from the stash Cibran had given them, moved the M4A1 aside and laid out a game of solitaire. It was going to be a long night.

CHAPTER 11

Nathan dozed fitfully, jerking awake at every strange sound. Conceding sleep as a lost cause, he rose and went to join Gabe in the main room.

Gabe had apparently given up on solitaire and moved on to card houses. Nathan tried to ignore the machine gun lying on the table. "Anything?"

Gabe shook his head. "People sneaking around. Nothing official. Like Cibran said, things should quiet down for a bit by morning. It will take the government a day or so to mobilize. That should give us a window to get out." His smile had a rueful twist. "I'm not really earning my retainer here."

Nathan shrugged. "I'm still alive, aren't I?"

"I'm also supposed to keep you out of danger, and I really haven't done that very well."

"Short of keeping me from coming up here in the first place and doing my job, I don't think there's anything you could have done to avoid this."

"You're quite calm about this all of a sudden."

"I'm not in a hole in the ground anymore. And I'm in good hands. Although I'm going to have to do something very nice for Cibran when we get out of here. And Alda."

"And Davi."

"That kid needs a good job. Or a good beating. I'm not sure which."

That earned him a smile, albeit fleeting.

He nodded at the haphazardly balanced cards. "Solitaire not cutting it anymore?"

Gabe shook his head. "You can only cheat so many times before it gets boring."

"There's two of us now. Poker?"

"I never win, remember?" Knocking over the cards, Gabe began to gather up the deck. "Five-card draw?"

"Strip poker."

"In the middle of what might as well be a war zone?"

"What, you have to be fully clothed to shoot someone?"

Gabe got a thoughtful look on his face that made Nathan suspicious. "*Have* you ever shot anyone in the altogether?"

"Does playing Halo in my boxers count?"

Nathan laughed. "No. Although I'd pay to see that." He took the cards from Gabe and continued righting them.

"You're not going to give me a choice in this, are you?"

"There's always a choice. Just say the word and we'll play Go Fish instead." He started shuffling the cards, letting a slow grin creep across his face. "What's the matter, Agent Callan, worried you won't be able to resist me if I lose my shirt?"

"I'm worried someone will break in here while I've got my pants around my knees and ruin a perfectly good erection."

"But it'd provide an excellent distraction. While they're looking at your impressive cock, it'll be easier to pull the gun on them."

"Oh, since your motives are entirely altruistic..." Gabe waved his hand. "Go ahead and deal."

The whole situation was surreal. Intellectually, Nathan had known kidnapping was a possibility, but hiring Gabe had been more in the lines of buying travel insurance when nothing was really likely to happen. He'd certainly never expected to be racing through the claustrophobic byways of Rio's slums with a pack of vengeance-minded drug runners after them, pissed off Nathan had tried to do some good. Getting Gabe naked seemed like the sanest thing he'd done all night.

By the fourth hand, it was Nathan who was sitting shirtless at the table, while Gabe had only forfeited his belt and right shoe.

"There's something distinctly unfair in all of this," Nathan said.

"It's not my fault the cards have been in my favor so far."

"I thought you said you never win."

"I did. You're just having a really crappy day."

"You aren't kidding."

After the tenth round, Nathan was left with only his black boxer-briefs. The only consolation was that Gabe had *finally* lost his shirt.

"You lied to me."

"Of course I lied to you. It's poker. You didn't expect me to tip my hand from the start, did you?" Gabe's eyes danced in the dim light. "I wouldn't have been much of an agent if I couldn't bluff, would I?"

Nathan threw down his cards. "Game change. Old Maid."

"Oh, no. We're playing this until someone wins."

"It's pretty obvious who that's going to be."

Gabe pursed his lips. "I suppose I'd be amenable to being convinced otherwise."

"You'd have to take off your goddamn pants for that."

Without missing a beat, Gabe undid his fly.

Nathan found himself licking his lips in anticipation. Jesus, he couldn't be any more obvious, could he?

Gabe left his fly open, his more salient attributes still hidden, as he tugged off his undershirt, revealing his broad chest to Nathan's hungry gaze. It was insane. Someone could break in any minute to kill them, but Nathan didn't care. Right now, here, he wanted to remember he was alive. And how alive this man made him feel.

Nathan knelt between Gabe's straddled legs, for the moment not caring how dirty the floorboards beneath his bare knees were.

"This is probably the stupidest thing we could be doing right now," Nathan said, even as he ran his palms lightly up Gabe's denim-clad thighs.

"It is, but I'm not exactly stopping you, am I?"

"Don't." He pulled Gabe's head down into a kiss, turning all the day's fear and frustration into aching need that he slipped into Gabe's mouth with his tongue.

Gabe didn't fight him, curving strong fingers around Nathan's head to hold him still as he returned the kiss, taking control of it, making it richer.

Nathan worked a hand into Gabe's open fly, stroking lightly along his erection, earning a hungry groan in response. "Take them off." Rationality was quickly sliding away, replaced with a desperate need to control Gabe, to fuck him, to ride him, to make him lose that iron restraint he'd worn all day.

Gabe obeyed, releasing Nathan's head to shove his jeans down, arching off the chair enough to grind his erection against Nathan's hip.

The fact anyone could walk in at any moment only made Nathan more desperate. "Want you so bad," he murmured against Gabe's hungry lips.

"Shhh." Gabe stroked Nathan's hair, comforting and arousing at once, even as his lips moved to tease the sensitive skin beneath his earlobe. "We've got time."

Nathan gradually slid back to his knees, nipping down the still pale skin of Gabe's chest. "We really need to get you some color."

"Fish-belly white doesn't appeal to you?"

"On you? Always. But I'm just imagining how good you'll taste warmed by the sun."

Gabe kept caressing Nathan's head, fingers tangling and combing through his hair in comfort and encouragement. His body was relaxed and open, his knees slightly splayed. "We are in Rio."

Nathan shook his head, making his lips tease across Gabe's nipple. "Not here. Barbados, maybe. Or Aruba."

"Ah, you're after a real vacation, I see."

Dipping his head, Nathan scented the length of Gabe's cock. "No work, no guard duty. Just two men enjoying the gorgeous weather."

"No one trying to kill us." Gabe's voice sounded rougher.

Good.

Nathan ran his tongue along the same path, finishing with a flourish around the head that made Gabe grunt. "Definitely."

"Although there's something to be said for the thrill of life and death situations."

Nathan sucked the tip of Gabe's cock past his lips, shaking his head as he tongued along the crease.

Gabe groaned and dropped his head back.

There was something dirty about the whole situation, Gabe sprawled in the hard little wooden chair, jeans around his ankles and a machine gun within easy reach, sidearm still holstered by his shoulder, while Nathan sucked him off. It was certainly more erotic than if they'd done the same in an armchair in the quiet safety of their hotel rooms. Maybe it was the adrenaline. Maybe it was the fear. Maybe it was just Gabe. Nathan didn't care.

Gabe tugged insistently on his hair, getting his attention.

Nathan glared up at him. "If someone's interrupting us, shoot them. Because I'm not stopping until I get you off."

"So you don't want to know there's a condom in my wallet."

"Well, okay, in that case you *can* interrupt me."

He fumbled around in the pile of Gabe's pants, never taking his mouth off his favorite new toy. He found the wallet and the condom in it by touch, never looking as he ripped it open and added it to his mouth play.

"Jesus. How did you learn to do that?"

"College." He let his fingers finish rolling it into place. "Safe sex parties."

"I went to the wrong college."

Grinning, Nathan kicked his shorts aside and moved astride Gabe's lap. "Good. It means there's plenty more I can show you."

Gabe folded his arms around him, gripping his ass for support and guidance. "I'm looking forward to it."

"God, so am I."

And then Nathan was easing down on Gabe's cock, the thin coating of lubricant barely enough to ease passage into Nathan's ass. Twice in one day was more than he'd hoped for. Or was it two days now?

Gabe supported him, and Nathan relaxed into his hold, using his straddling legs and the resistance of Gabe's embrace to rise up and slowly sink down again. He was so full, Gabe felt so good inside him, and more than anything he felt safe.

They built to a steady pace, exchanging kisses and swallowing each other's groans of pleasure.

Nathan clutched the chair back behind Gabe's shoulders for support, for leverage, as he buried his face in Gabe's shoulder, lost in the slap of sweat-coated skin and the fricative drag of skin and latex. He should be worried about the stability of the chair, but he wasn't, slamming onto Gabe harder and harder until he came, startling himself.

Gabe stood up, still gripping Nathan, still buried in him and carried him to the bed. Nathan clung to him with the last of his strength, grateful to give control over to his lover.

The bed wasn't much sturdier than the chair as Gabe fucked Nathan into the threadbare mattress. Nathan didn't care. He dug blunt nails into Gabe's back, urging him on, until Gabe came with a cry muffled against Nathan's shoulder.

There wasn't enough room in the narrow bed for them to lie side by side, but Gabe managed to turn and tangle them so they fit comfortably, his arms around Nathan and his breath huffing in his ear. "Go to sleep for a while. I'll be here."

The last thing Nathan wanted to do was sleep, but with his body sated and mind quiet, not to mention Gabe curled protectively around him, he stood little chance of resisting.

CHAPTER 12

Nathan dropped off to sleep quickly, and it was tempting to follow after him. Instead, Gabe eased himself out of the bed and returned to the front room.

He pulled his pants on and checked the door and windows. No movement outside, although he could make out just the palest hints off dawn over the tattered roofs around them. Another hour or so and Cibran would be there, hopefully to lead them closer to safety.

He returned to the bedroom just as Nathan started to stir. Sitting up, Nathan glared at him. "You really have to stop doing that."

Gabe leaned against the doorframe. "What? Slipping out while you're asleep?"

"Yes."

"Sorry, it's in the job description. You might want to get dressed. Cibran should be here soon." He tossed Nathan his clothes and started buttoning up his own shirt, gun and holster back in place.

Nathan sorted through the pile for his underwear. "I don't know, I'm starting to get sentimental about this place. Why don't we just stay here?"

"Because there are still bad men with guns out there. And you haven't had to use the facilities yet."

Wrinkling his nose, Nathan tugged on his underwear, then his pants. "You may have a point there."

The "facilities" were a coffee can in the corner of the bedroom. Gabe could see Nathan trying not to think about it too much.

They were just finishing off the last of the bottled water and a handful of trail mix when a light tap sounded at the window. Gabe stiffened, hand going to his pistol. The tap came again at the door. "It's me," Cibran's voice came through the thin metal. "Don't shoot. I'm coming in."

He ducked in, giving them both a once-over, gaze settling on Gabe's recently-acquired gun. "Moving up in the world, I see."

Gabe turned the machine gun over in his hand. "I'd give it to you, but I think I'm going to need it. Piece in a puzzle."

"What puzzle?"

"I'm not sure. I haven't found the edges of it yet."

Cibran seemed confused by that, but he let it pass. "Things have quieted down, so we can move you. You are almost to Chapeu Mangueira here." Gabe recognized the name as another of the nearby *favelas*. "From there, we should be able to smuggle you down into the Praca Julio de Noron and then back to safety. But we'll have to move carefully and stay out of sight. It is harder by day than under cover of night."

"I suppose it's too much to hope maybe the drug lords have gone to sleep," Nathan ventured.

Cibran gave him a tight smile. "I would not count on it. But hoping is fine."

Gabe stuffed the cards and the empty bottles back in the knapsack and slung it over his shoulder, the M4A1 going over the other shoulder. He thought for a moment, then offered Cibran his Beretta.

Cibran took the weapon, handling it like an old lover. Double-checking the safety, he then secured it in his waistband. "Such a good weapon. Are you sure you wish to part with it?"

"I might hesitate if it were my personal one, but as I obtained it locally, I have no sentimental attachment."

"This I can understand. Still, I thank you." He made his way to the door. "Follow me, stay low and keep quiet."

Gabe let Nathan follow, then came after, closing the door behind them. No point in leaving any sign they'd been there. Cibran might need the place again.

They made their way carefully through the neighborhood, although there was more life in it than they had seen the day before. People were moving about, collecting water, running errands, even a few children were out playing. None of them looked at Gabe and his machine gun. *Don't get involved.* He could almost see it on everyone's faces.

Their journey out of the *favela* went smoothly, almost too smoothly for Gabe's comfort. So he was somewhat relieved when they encountered a patrol on the outskirts, taking refuge in scrub in the nick of time.

Cibran held them back. "Let them pass. They aren't looking for you, just minding the passages. They'll be gone in a minute."

Gabe could hear traffic not too far off in the distance. "I'm going to need a bag or a blanket before we get into civilized territory. I can't just carry this into the hotel." He gestured with the machine gun.

"No, not if you wish to go home soon. We'll look."

Once the guards had passed, the trio continued on their way. Cibran drew them up short in the shadows of one of the nicer looking shacks they passed. "Less than a minute. Keep out of sight." Then he left them.

"I think this was less nerve-wracking when freedom didn't seem to so close," Nathan murmured.

He was more right than he knew.

Cibran returned to them carrying a duffle just large enough to fit the gun and their few remaining supplies. "The knapsack is nicer. It is a fair trade," he explained as he set it by the side of the *favela.* "Ready?"

The last shanties jutted out from a rock outcropping just over a well-paved two-lane road. Cibran gestured beyond it. "That is the *praca.* Beyond that, you can see the hotels. The park should be safe, but if you don't trust it, make for the beach."

Nathan looked concerned. "What about you?"

Cibran shrugged. "I'm just another *favelado.* No one will notice me."

Nathan didn't seem happy with that answer, but he offered his hand, and Cibran took it. "Be careful, my friend," he insisted. "I'll be back and looking for you."

"I'm quite looking forward to a roof that doesn't leak." With a wink, Cibran left them.

"Ready?" Gabe asked.

Nathan nodded. "As I'll ever be."

It was twenty feet down a sheer rock face to the road below. But there was no helping it. Gabe slung the duffle onto his back like a backpack and braced himself at the edge. "You first."

Nathan looked over the edge. "That's a long way down."

"It's either that or back to the shanty for a few months while the military gets their act together."

Nathan gave him a dirty look. "It had a coffee can for a toilet."

"Then this is better, isn't it?"

"I hate you." But he took Gabe's hands and lowered himself over the edge.

Between Nathan's height and Gabe's reach, they got him about halfway down. "Just slide. Don't try to stop it or control it, just keep yourself straight and upright. And bend your knees when you get to the bottom."

"Christ, skydiving was less terrifying."

"Well, the parachute kind of helps."

"Funny man." Taking a deep breath and blowing it out, Nathan let go.

He couldn't have followed Gabe's instructions more perfectly. Gabe grinned and went after Nathan before he could think twice.

His descent went well until the bottom. Either he'd misjudged or just been too slow, hitting the ground harder than he'd anticipated, knees giving way completely. Well, that sucked.

A hand appeared in his line of sight. "Need a hand?"

"Yes, I looked like an idiot," Gabe grumbled and let Nathan pull him to his feet, then almost went down again when his left ankle gave a sharp stab of pain. "Fuck."

Nathan slung Gabe's arm around his shoulder and supported him as they gimped past a line of buses to a cabstand not fifty feet from the most famous beach in the world. The whole thing was surreal.

Gabe kept the bag at his feet as Nathan gave the driver the name of their hotel. The man looked at them suspiciously, but pulled away from the curb. Only then did Gabe relax.

Nathan slumped in the seat next to him. "Shower. Meat. Sleep. Mostly in that order."

There would be more. But for now Gabe thought that was a pretty good list.

CHAPTER 13

Nathan took the opportunity to shower while Gabe was getting checked over by the hotel physician, at Nathan's insistence.

"It's a sprain. He's going to tell me it's a sprain. What's the point?"

"Humor me?"

Gabe had protested heartily, but went along with it in the end.

The hot, pelting water was the best thing Nathan had possibly ever experienced.

Part of him felt guilty. He thought of Alda and Cibran and Davi, still stuck up on the side of that mountain in their tiny shacks, no running water at all, let alone hot water, surrounded by people who would kill them if they found out what they'd done. But every part of him ached, and he had abrasions on his ass and shoulders that stung as soap ran down his back into them, and he was alive.

Alive was good. And guilt he could deal with. If nothing else, he was more determined than ever to get his micro-housing established here. These people deserved a better life.

His heart nearly stopped when the shower curtain was tugged aside.

Gabe grinned and carefully eased himself into the tub behind Nathan.

"Shouldn't you be elevating your ankle or something?"

"Eventually. But I'll be much more amenable to sitting around on my ass once I'm clean."

"What about using your own shower?"

"It's lacking one important feature."

"Oh?"

"You."

Nathan didn't stop Gabe from folding himself around him. Frankly, the contact was more than welcome. "You just want me to hold you up."

"Among other things." Gabe had his face buried in Nathan's neck, his words vibrating off Nathan's wet skin.

"Wash first."

Gabe grumbled into his shoulder.

"You'll feel better for it."

"Fine." He leaned back and let the water run over him, sliding between their bodies as Gabe refused to give up his hold on Nathan. It was tempting to turn around and watch the patterns the water made as it skated over his lover's body, but Nathan preferred the physical to the visual, at least at the moment.

Gabe tipped his head forward again, raining water over Nathan's shoulder and chest. "Better?"

"Soap."

Gabe sighed, but reached for the hotel issue bar in the soap tray. "You want to do the honors?"

"You sprained your ankle, not your arms," Nathan groused, but still took the bar from Gabe and faced him properly. "Turn around."

"You just want to look at my ass."

"That goes without saying."

Gabe obliged, bracing against the wall, as Nathan soaped up his hands and began to map the broad planes. He scrubbed at dirt and sweat, but also worked tension out of the muscles as best he could in their present position. "I'll do more later," he promised.

"Don't spoil me. I'll get used to it."

"And that's a bad thing?"

"I think our two weeks got cut a bit short."

"Don't think about that now."

Gabe had the same scrapes on his shoulders and backside Nathan did, nothing bleeding or raw, just roughed patches that exposed the more tender skin beneath. Nathan washed around those carefully, but was very attentive to other, more intimate places until Gabe's groans were echoing off the tiles.

"Turn around," he ordered, and Gabe obeyed, leaning back. He was well on his way to hard. "Oh, yes, very nice."

Nathan took his time, washing Gabe's chest with as much care as his back. Finishing with Gabe's stomach, Nathan bypassed his obvious erection and began to soap Gabe's legs. First right, then left, taking extra care with his ankle.

"You're torturing me on purpose."

"I think that's rather obvious."

Gabe caught Nathan by the back of the neck and drew him up to a kiss, their bodies frictionless against each other through the soap. By the time Gabe released him, Nathan was whimpering and hard. Gabe chuckled. "Now we're even."

Nathan slithered his hand through the soap that lingered on Gabe's thigh and wrapped it around Gabe's cock. "Not for long."

Gabe's eyes drifted closed and he arched into Nathan's touch. "I'm fine with that."

"I know you are." Then he pulled them both under the spray to rinse off. Soap gone, he turned off the water and tugged the curtain back. "But we're going to do this somewhere a lot less wet where your ankle won't give out just as things are getting good."

Drying off included as much tongue as towel, but by the time they made it to Nathan's bed, they were dry enough not to soak the sheets. Gabe moved to cover him, but Nathan resisted, slipping his hand between Gabe's thighs to finger his perineum. "You mind if I have a turn?"

Gabe relaxed back against the pillows. "Not at all."

Nathan got up again to fetch the condoms and lube he'd put in Gabe's room the morning before all hell had broken loose. He set them on the nightstand, as if throwing down a gauntlet, daring Gabe to go through them all.

Gabe raised an eyebrow before sitting up and taking one of the rubbers out of the box. He carefully tore it open, tossed away the wrapper and, never breaking eye contact with Nathan, put it in his mouth.

Nathan groaned.

Gabe's mouth felt incredible as he wrapped it around Nathan's cock, but his oral dexterity was unfortunately lacking. By the time he gave up trying, they were both laughing. "I'll get it, I promise," he said, rolling the condom in place the old fashioned way.

Nathan pressed him back onto the bed. "I'm looking forward to you practicing."

"So am I." With a wicked smirk, Gabe picked up the bottle of lube and squeezed out a generous amount. But instead of applying it directly to Nathan's cock as he'd expected, Gabe reached between his own legs and began to finger himself open.

Nathan very nearly lost it. "You're doing that on purpose."

"Am I?"

"Yes, you are." Nathan caught Gabe's wrist and brought the slippery hand to his cock, rolling his head back as Gabe slicked him up.

"You want this so bad." It wasn't a question.

Nathan fucked Gabe's hand. "So do you."

"Yeah, I do." Using his grip, he pulled Nathan down, splaying his knees to give him better access.

And then Nathan was pressing in, Gabe's muscles easing up just enough to let him in, but still tight and so hot. It was almost too much. "Fuck me."

"Oh no, it's your turn, remember?" But Gabe's voice had a rough edge, revealing he wasn't completely unaffected either.

"Oh, I remember." He began moving, slowly, aware of every point of contact between them. "I remember everything about you, Gabriel Callan."

Gabe gripped Nathan's forearms, head grinding back into the pillows. "Tell me."

So he did, driving home every few words with a harder thrust.

"I remember how you showed up for our first meeting twenty minutes late. I could tell Jeannie had just straightened your hair and your tie, and I wanted to muss them up again."

"That was CTA's fault."

"And I'm probably the only person grateful for that." He licked a wide stripe of Gabe's throat. "Then there was the plane ride, where you couldn't sit still, couldn't stop looking at me."

"You looked so comfortable in your skin."

Gabe looked so debauched right now, and Nathan knew it was because of him. "And you were wearing that stupid fucking suit, like you were still with the agency instead of with me."

"Easier to play the part when you dress it."

"Then you should be naked all the goddamn time." He was losing the threads of his control, unwinding a little more with every stroke.

"Most of my clients wouldn't be so understanding."

"I'm sure Jeannie would be amused."

Gabe dragged him down into a hungry kiss. "Don't you dare mention it to her. I'll never hear the end of it."

"Her loss. My gain. Christ, Gabe!"

Neither of them was all that capable of speech after that, the frenetic pace driving them higher. When Gabe began stroking himself in time with Nathan's thrusts, it just about did Nathan in.

He wrapped his fingers around Gabe's, burying his face in Gabe's neck. "Christ, Gabe, kill me. Kill me right now. I don't want there to be a more perfect moment than this."

"But there will be."

He came so hard the world went white.

Gabe was wrapped tightly around him when Nathan returned to his senses, the wetness quickly cooling between them indicating Gabe had found release as well.

As his heart slowed and breathing calmed, Nathan finally registered his last words. "Now you can kill me. Saying I love you would have been less humiliating."

Gabe chuckled. "I think it's still early for any grand declarations, but I promise not to tell anyone. And if I do, you've got plenty of fodder to give to Jeannie to make me miserable."

"Well, that's a relief." Nathan withdrew from Gabe and flopped onto his back. "Maybe it's a good thing we won't be here for the two weeks. Neither of us would survive it."

"Certainly not with our dignity intact." Gabe sat up with a groan.

Nathan caught his arm. "Where are you going?"

"To wrap up my ankle and then make calls to the local police and the U.S. Embassy. We have to report what happened. If nothing else, your local sponsors will have reported our disappearance."

"Maybe we should stay missing for a while. Might get the problems down here on the evening news for a few days."

"It might also make it hard to expense a couple of days' worth of room service." He kissed Nathan again, in a light and affectionate way, before getting up to hobble back to his room.

Nathan watched him go. A couple days of room service didn't sound like a bad idea. Perhaps once they wrapped things up here in Rio, Gabe might be amenable to taking a vacation somewhere with plenty of sand and a long way away from drug cartels and anything work related for either of them.

Hauling himself out of the bed, Nathan ducked in the bathroom to clean up, then returned and buried himself under the covers. Gabe could deal with the real world right now if he wanted, but Nathan was going to put it off just a bit longer.

That the bed smelled like both of them only added to the fact he didn't want to leave it any time soon.

CHAPTER 14

Gabe let Nathan sleep. Frankly, it was a temptation to join him. But this was the shit he was getting paid for, so sleep was at least a few hours off for him yet.

Once his ankle was wrapped, he picked up the phone.

His first call was to the consulate. It took a while to get through to the right desk and then he had to repeat the story twice. In the end, it saved him the second call to the local constabulary, as the State Department official agreed to handle the Brazilian authorities. They made an appointment for him and Nathan to meet with the consular rep and the police at the same time the next morning to give their statements. The rep assured Gabe that they could be on a plane back to the States within three days.

He ordered a good old American cheeseburger and fries from room service before making his next call.

"Callan Securities, this is Jeannie Murray."

"Hey, hon."

"Gabe! Jesus Christ, where the hell are you?"

"Back in my hotel room for the first time in a few days."

"What happened?"

Gabe's lips twisted, only partly in amusement. "I got laid. Drug lords decided to take back the *favela* Nathan was inspecting, so we got to experience life in the Rio slums firsthand. Found out the drug lords have someone in the US backing them. Won at strip poker. Got laid. Escaped. Twisted my ankle. Had a shower. Got laid. Dealt with two countries' bureaucracies. Called my business partner and ex to check in. Hoping to get laid again after a good night's sleep."

"Back up a second there. You won at poker?"

"Way to focus on the important things, Jeannie."

"Well, the getting laid was a foregone conclusion. Once you got over yourself." Sobering, she asked, "How do you know someone from the States is helping the drug lords?"

Gabe unzipped the duffle bag and pulled out the gun. "Oh, because I just happen to have a brand new model M4A1 I got off one of the grunts."

Jeannie whistled. "Those aren't easy to come by."

"Not by us. Fortunately, whoever procured them must not have been very hands-on because the serial number's still here. Got a pen?"

"Of course."

Gabe rattled off the long string of numbers and letters, and Jeannie dutifully repeated it back to him.

"Find out who ordered those and where they were intended. I don't think the State Department's going to be too happy with someone smuggling high tech weaponry to low rent drug cartels, especially with the Olympics in the offing."

"Yeah, that wouldn't look good."

"Not to mention really bad form."

"It wouldn't be the first time."

"That's just what the US needs right now, another Iran-Contra."

"Fan-fucking-tastic." Jeannie sighed. "As soon as I find out something, I'll let you know."

"Thanks, Jeannie. Nathan and I are meeting with a rep from the consulate and the police tomorrow morning first thing, so if you turn anything up…"

"When I know, you'll know."

He sighed. "Take your time. I'm going to sleep for about ten hours."

"Not with Nathan around, you aren't." He could hear the grin in her voice.

"He's already out cold. I think I'm safe. I'll call you when I get up."

"Promises, promises."

Once he hung up, Gabe looked at his empty bed. The smart thing to do would be to crawl under the covers and die for the next half a day.

Walking over, he opened the door between their rooms. Nathan lay on his side, out for the count. But there was just enough space beside him…

"Man up," he told himself. Nathan would likely come and bug him anyway once he woke up. Might as well face the inevitable sooner rather than later. At least this way he might get more rest.

Gabe tossed his robe over the nearby armchair and climbed into the bed beside Nathan.

Nathan let out a soft sigh, and Gabe surrendered completely, sliding his arm around Nathan's waist to curl up against his back.

"I could get used to this," Nathan mumbled.

"Go back to sleep," Gabe murmured against his ear, but Nathan already had, if indeed he'd ever been awake at all. Gabe nestled in closer, letting the soporific heat from Nathan's body seep into him and drag him down as well.

*   *   *

Someone was watching him. Gabe peeked an eye open and found that someone was Nathan. "Could you stare a little less obviously? Some of us are still catching up on our sleep."

Nathan grinned. "I'm not used to falling asleep alone and waking up to find someone else in my bed."

"Me, neither. Which is why I crashed here rather than possibly murdering you when you snuck into my bed later."

"So this was for my own good."

Gabe closed his eyes again, but couldn't help a small smile. "Yup."

He became aware of Nathan's light touch, his fingers tracing idle patterns along his torso.

"What are you doing?"

"Making sure you're really here."

"I really am. And I'm also really wanting to sleep."

He didn't need to see Nathan to know the man was grinning. "Don't mind me."

Warm lips on his chest guaranteed that wasn't going to happen. "What time is it?"

"Almost six." Nathan's mouth didn't stop plying Gabe's skin.

Gabe was surprised. He'd been out almost seven hours. He didn't usually sleep so heavily. Certainly not with someone else in the bed. "Don't you have some calls to make?"

Nathan looked up, resting his chin on Gabe's chest. "You sound like you don't want me here."

"I'd have slept in my own bed if that were the case."

"You may have a point."

"May?"

Nathan nodded, then resumed his exploration. "As for the calls, I already took care of them. Or my assistant is. You handled the consulate, so there really wasn't much left for me to do."

"Other than wake me up."

"Mmm. Other than wake you up."

He couldn't even pretend to be mad, and he certainly wasn't going back to sleep.

Not that he really wanted to. He tugged on Nathan's short hair. "Come here."

Nathan shook his head, chin bumping against the head of Gabe's cock. "No way. I'm exactly where I want to be."

"You're orally fixated." He forced Nathan back up and rolled him beneath him. "You don't have to do that every time we're together."

Nathan's hands caressed over Gabe's back and ass, touching every part of him as Nathan wound around him. "Maybe I like to."

"Well, maybe I'd like a chance."

Nathan grinned. "Far be it from me to stop you. I'm well-rested, so no fear I'll fall asleep."

"How is it that always comes off like an insult to me?"

It was hard to concentrate with the way Nathan was twined around him, touching every part of him. Nathan licked along Gabe's throat, making him shudder. "No insult intended. I still kick myself for not having better stamina."

"The wine at dinner didn't help."

"You wouldn't let me have any more coffee. And it would have been rude to refuse."

Gabe caught Nathan's wrists and pinned his arms above his head, eliciting a satisfying groan. Encouraged, Gabe rocked his hips in a slow, steady rhythm, their cocks rubbing against each other enough to make Gabe ache. "The coffee wouldn't have done you any good. Considering how much you'd had, another cup or two wouldn't have changed things."

"It might have bought me a few more minutes to enjoy things."

"Or had us experiencing Brazilian healthcare firsthand."

Nathan was twisting beneath him, making it hard for Gabe to retain his composure. He bent down to brush his lips against Nathan's ear. "Besides, wasn't it worth the wait?"

"Fuck, yes." Nathan arched up into him. "Though, I'm not a fan of waiting right now."

"Say please."

"Please."

"Please what?"

"Please suck me off."

"No, Nathan." Gabe scented along Nathan's neck, brushing all the sensitive places he'd memorized in the past few days. "Beg me. Beg me to lick you and swallow you and suck your balls and finger your ass until you're begging me to fuck you. If you can talk at all at that point."

"Jesus…" He felt Nathan swallow hard. "Can't really talk now."

Gabe laughed. "*Beg* me, Nathan."

"Please, Gabe." His voice was cracking already. "Please, oh, Christ, please do it."

Gabe was enjoying this too much. He tightened his grip on Nathan's arms. "Not good enough."

"You're inhuman." Nathan licked his lips and locked his gaze with Gabe's. "Suck me off and swallow me down and finger me until I can't think straight. *Please*, Gabe."

"Good boy." *Thank fuck.* He moved down Nathan's body, licking, sucking, biting, Nathan's erection prodding at his chest the whole way. The sound Nathan made when Gabe finally took him in his mouth was quite possibly the most gratifying thing he'd ever heard.

Gabe took his time, tasting cock, balls, the skin around and behind. Nathan's legs splayed wider, making it easier for Gabe to take whatever he wanted, and his fingers clenched in the mattress, fighting whatever urges he had to grab Gabe's head, make him go faster, harder, deeper, anything.

So Gabe drew things out, going slower, thoroughly exploring every inch Nathan had on offer.

"Fuck me." It came out breathless.

Gabe could get off on making Nathan come undone.

He shook his head, Nathan's cock still in his mouth. Nathan gasped.

He worked two fingers into Nathan's hole, sucking him hard the entire time. Nathan whimpered.

He pressed hard on a single, familiar spot. With a roar, Nathan exploded.

Gabe took everything he had and sought more.

He waited for Nathan to recover his senses, grabbing a condom from the nightstand and sliding it on. When Nathan opened his eyes again, Gabe shoved one leg back, pinning Nathan's wrists again with his free hand and probing for entry. By now, his cock ached and his reason was fading under the pounding drumbeat of desperation he had generated in himself by driving Nathan out of his mind. He needed this, now.

He thrust forward. Nathan cried out, joyous.

Now Gabe went for hard and fast, satisfying his own overwhelming need.

Nathan held him, gripped Gabe's hips with his thighs, murmured filthy encouragement into Gabe's ear until all he could think about was how Nathan felt, how he smelled, how he tasted. Gabe gripped Nathan's ass tighter and fucked him harder.

When he finally came, it was exquisite.

He lay there in Nathan's embrace, recovering.

Nathan's lips brushed against his temple. "Aren't you glad I woke you up?"

"If you hadn't fallen asleep the other night, we could've been doing this for days."

"No, we couldn't. We were hiding from drug lords for two days, remember?"

"And yet we still managed."

"Yeah." Nathan settled down next to him. "We're pretty good that way."

Gabe couldn't disagree.

"And for the record, this isn't ending here in Rio," Nathan said definitively. "We'll figure out logistics and everything else when we come to it. But we will be pursuing this somewhere, somehow. Got it?"

Baltimore and Chicago were hardly next door to each other, so it definitely would be tricky. But hopefully worth it. "What if I say no?"

Nathan shook his head. "You aren't going to say no."

Gabe pulled him closer. "I'm not going to say no." He kissed Nathan's forehead. "Now go to sleep. Bureaucrats in the morning."

"Don't like bureaucrats." Nathan was already half asleep.

"Then you got into the wrong line of work."

"Like you."

Gabe couldn't argue with that, either.

CHAPTER 15

Nathan hated bureaucracy. He hated it even more when said bureaucracy took up the better part of his day.

The meeting with the State Department official and the police went on for hours, trapping them in uncomfortable plastic chairs, which had been stylish back in 1957. Between the two organizations, Nathan and Gabe had to present every piece of documentation they had to prove they were in the country and the *favela* legitimately. Gabe had hidden the machine gun in his room or Nathan was sure there would be more questions. Then they had just enough time to stuff down a quick lunch before Nathan had to meet with his backers at the hotel.

It was well into dinnertime when Nathan's obligations finally wrapped up. More than anything, it made him appreciate Terry all the more for handling the bulk of this. Gabe, unfortunately, had to deal with his red tape on his own, leaving Nathan to his own devices and with a State Department guard on the door.

Nathan was indulging in room service when he heard Gabe curse loudly in his room. Nathan hadn't even realized he was back.

He went to the door. "What's wrong?" Gabe paced the floor, and it wasn't until he turned that Nathan saw the phone at his ear. Gabe held up a finger to forestall him as he continued his conversation. "Are you sure?" After a moment, Gabe muttered, "That son of a bitch. Yeah, we're clear to leave any time. First flight out, if you can manage. Thanks, Jeannie."

Nathan stood there, waiting.

"Deguerre," was Gabe's response.

"Is the son of a bitch? Okay, no surprise there."

"No, the gun was purchased by Dagger Securities. Meaning Deguerre funded the little takeover of the *favela* we recently escaped."

"He... What? Why would he do that?"

"Better business for big dogs like him if the drug lords are back in control because it gives him more leverage to obtain certain contracts."

"In other words, screw you over."

"A definite side benefit."

"But he couldn't have known we'd make it out of there in one piece."

"Oh, I think he was counting on the opposite."

Nathan wasn't an innocent by any means. In his line of work, he knew the lengths people would go to to remain on top, be they governments or corporations or local wannabe rulers. But this was beyond the pale. It shouldn't be a surprise after all Haliburton had done in the Middle East—that people were aware of—but... "Son of a bitch."

"Exactly."

"So what happens now?"

"Now you go home, and I stay here and start an international incident. I have to turn the machine gun over to the consulate and turn in all our information on Dagger."

Nathan gaped at him. "Go home? I'm the reason we're here in the first place."

"Nathan, there's nothing you can do. I'm the one with the government background. They're going to want me here to give statements to a dozen different agencies. And I'm going to have to explain why I didn't turn in the M4A1 when we first talked to the State Department. There's nothing you can do here."

"No."

"Nathan—"

He cut Gabe off. "I've still got work I can do here in Rio. No, I'm not planning on going up to the *favelas* again. At least not in the near future. But there's plenty I can do to lay the groundwork to help those people before I can actually help them."

Gabe's jaw tightened. "It's not safe for you here anymore. You charged me with your safety. That's first priority, so you're going home."

"Then I'm terminating the contract."

"Then I'll have the State boys ship you out. You aren't staying here, Nathan."

Nathan was pretty sure Gabe wasn't bluffing. "Call the State boys. That's the only way I'm leaving before you do."

Gabe didn't hesitate, dialing the phone with sure fingers.

Nathan stood his ground. "I'm not fooling around."

"I know you're not. And neither am I."

"God damn it, Gabe!" He snatched the phone out of Gabe's hand and disconnected it. "I'm not a goddamn maiden in distress. You can't shelter me."

"I'm not sheltering you. I'm making sure you don't get killed because some asshole with too much pull is gunning for me."

"I think I should be the one to make that decision, don't you?"

"Obviously I don't. Now get packed."

One of them was going to have to give or they'd be standing here until the end of time.

"You are a stubborn son of a bitch, Gabriel Callan. Is that why Jeannie divorced you?"

"It's what kept us together as long as we were. I refused to admit the truth."

"Like now?"

"Nathan—"

Nathan stepped close enough to caress Gabe's chest. "I can't go now. There won't be any flights until tomorrow. Are you going to hold out on me until then?"

Gabe caught his wrist, but he wore the faintest hint of a smile. "Don't think you can charm your way out of this with your masculine wiles, Nathan."

"Maybe I just want to take advantage of you while I can."

"It'll be easier to take advantage of me when I'm not worrying about whether or not we're both about to get killed."

"Not so easy if I'm in Baltimore and you're here." If he was going to surrender, he was getting his pound of flesh out of it first. He teased his lips along Gabe's jaw, enjoying the faint tremor it generated.

"Christ, you're insatiable," Gabe murmured, tugging him closer.

"I am, and you'd damned well better get used to it."

If he was going to have to suffer without Gabe, then he was going to make sure Gabe suffered as well.

176

CHAPTER 16

It was a miserable three weeks. Gabe spent every day of them trapped in Rio, a virtual prisoner in his hotel, while a line of State Department officials and Brazilian bureaucrats filed through with questions and accusations. Once Interpol showed up, it only got worse.

The only good thing was that Nathan was clear of it. He hadn't been the one to withhold evidence in an international investigation. Their last night together had been memorable. The next morning had been as well, in a purely masochistic way. He had been able to walk Nathan as far as the lobby, where a black sedan from the consulate waited for him.

But now Gabe was back home as well, or nearly so. The tarmac at O'Hare was as good as home. At least until he was through the interminable wait while the plane taxied to the gate and the passengers could hurry up and wait to disembark.

Jeannie met him herself, wrapping her arms around him. "Welcome home."

He hugged her back, grateful for human contact. "It's good to be back."

She took his duffle from him. "Let's get you home."

The ride to his loft was quiet on his end, with Jeannie filling in the silence with the more mundane aspects of business and life. Until she said, "I'm seeing someone."

Jeannie had dated plenty since the divorce and rarely felt the need to tell him details, all the while prying into his.

"Must be serious."

"There's potential for serious."

"Have you checked him out?"

She shot him a dirty look.

"Right, I forgot who I was talking about. Of course you did."

"It just seemed like, since you were finally getting on with your life, I should get on with mine."

"A few days in Rio hardly counts as moving on."

"Right. When did you last talk to Nathan?"

"I haven't talked to him since he came home." Which was true. They hadn't talked. But he'd gotten enough dirty texts and naked pictures of Nathan to raise a few eyebrows with his State Department handlers and provide him plenty of masturbation fodder. He hadn't been able to bring himself to do the same in return.

His more standard texts, few as he'd sent, seemed to have satisfied Nathan enough to keep responding.

"So you won't mind, then, that I gave him the key to your place when he flew in."

He was glad Jeannie was the one driving. "Nathan's here?"

She grinned. "Got in this morning."

Well...hell. "Seriously?"

With a sigh, she pulled to the side of the interstate, flipping on the emergency blinkers. Then she faced him. "Gabriel Callan, don't you dare start panicking now."

"I'm not panicking!" *Much.* His heart really shouldn't be beating *that* fast, should it?

"You are. I saw it often enough when we started dating."

"And look how well it turned out."

One of her eyebrows arched up.

"That's not what I meant."

"I know it isn't." Jeannie gave him a soft, fleeting smile. "Although, maybe I should have warned Nathan. Once you get over the initial freak out, he's going to be stuck with you."

"If he's already here, do you really think he's going to take no for an answer?"

Now she grinned. "How do you think I got you?"

"If he's got you on his side, I really don't stand a chance."

"Nope, so sit back and enjoy the ride."

He wanted to, but he was surprised to find himself anxious about seeing Nathan again. Nathan had been adamant in Rio, but then that had been Rio, a world away. After all this time, things wouldn't be the same between them. They couldn't be.

Jeannie had the car several miles down the freeway before he fully realized they were moving again.

"Stop over-thinking every little thing, Gabe. It'll be fine."

"Fine." Right.

*　　*　　*

"Are you sure you don't want to come in?" Gabe asked as Jeannie idled the car in front of his building.

"I'd love to come in, but I really don't think you're quite ready for a voyeur. Yet. Nathan, however…"

Leaning over, he kissed her on the cheek. "You're an amazing woman, and I don't deserve you."

"Sure you do. That's why we're partners. But you need this, too."

"Thanks." Steeling himself, Gabe grabbed his bag and got out of the car.

He heard the window power down as he started up the sidewalk. "A little less dead man walking and a bit more I'm going to get laid strut."

Before he could comment, Jeannie zoomed off.

The light was on in his condo. So much for the faint hope Nathan had chickened out. Not that it was likely. Nathan was pretty fearless. And very determined.

He tightened his hold on the bag and went in.

Riding up in the elevator seemed to take an eternity. So much for hi-speed. When it finally reached his floor, Gabe stood there and didn't exit until the doors started to close. A few short steps and he was in front of his own door. Did he use his key and enter like he didn't know Nathan was there? Or did he knock? And who the hell knocked on their own door?

Nathan, once again, decided things for him. He leaned in the now open doorway. "Good thing Jeannie gave me a heads up. I thought she was joking when she told me you'd vacillate forever before coming in."

"Yeah, well, she's got a lot to answer for. Hello, Nathan."

He answered with a smile, his bright eyes crinkling. "Hello, Gabriel. Welcome home."

"Thanks. I think."

Nathan still looked amused. "You planning to stand out in the hall all night?"

179

"Maybe."

Nathan came out, came close enough Gabe could feel his warmth. "What are you so afraid of?"

Why lie? "The real world isn't Rio, and my track record isn't exactly stellar."

"I don't know...the fact you and your ex-wife not only work together but seem to still genuinely care about what happens to the other says otherwise."

"That's different. Jeannie—"

"I get it. Jeannie's a great girl, and your relationship with her is all heteronormative. I'm your first real relationship on this side of the fence and you aren't sure what the hell you're doing. Am I right?"

That made Gabe smile. "To be fair, I didn't really know what I was doing on the other side of the fence, either."

Nathan nodded. "That explains so much."

"Smartass."

Taking Gabe's duffle, he motioned inside the condo. "First things first. Come inside so I can properly ravage you. We'll figure out the rest from there."

"Don't you think we should talk first?"

He gave Gabe a gentle shove. "If there's one thing I've learned about you, Gabriel Callan, it's that you're a man of action. So, action first, and if you can still think straight when I'm done with you, then we can talk. But I wouldn't count on that."

Gabe went inside. "Don't get used to it, though."

"What?"

"Bossing me around."

"Oh, I haven't even started."

The door closed behind them with a satisfying click. One thing it wouldn't be was boring. Gabe could live with that.

India Harper

India Harper is the combined persona of Philippa Grey-Gerou and Emery Sanborne. Emery and Grey have been writing solo for five years and together for even longer, resulting in a dozen works in the hetero and ménage genres. As they already share a brain, they figured it was high time to share a name as well. Their stories under the name India Harper have a slightly harder edge as they explore predominately male/male relationships in the rich environments of Philadelphia and Pittsburgh. Emery lives in Philadelphia with her cat, while Grey lives in the Philadelphia suburbs with a less well-behaved zoo.

AMBER QUILL PRESS, LLC
THE GOLD STANDARD IN PUBLISHING

QUALITY BOOKS
IN BOTH PRINT AND ELECTRONIC FORMATS

ACTION/ADVENTURE	SUSPENSE/THRILLER
SCIENCE FICTION	DARK FANTASY
MAINSTREAM	ROMANCE
HORROR	EROTICA
FANTASY	GLBT
WESTERN	MYSTERY
PARANORMAL	HISTORICAL
YOUNG ADULT	NON-FICTION

AMBER QUILL PRESS, LLC
http://www.amberquill.com

Made in the USA
Lexington, KY
14 December 2011